A KNIFE
IN THE BACK

Also by Bill Crider

A Knife
in the Back

Bill Crider

THOMAS DUNNE BOOKS
ST. MARTIN'S MINOTAUR
NEW YORK

THOMAS DUNNE BOOKS.
An imprint of St. Martin's Press.

A KNIFE IN THE BACK. Copyright © 2002 by Bill Crider. All rights reserved.
Printed in the United States of America. No part of this book may be used
or reproduced in any manner whatsoever without written permission
except in the case of brief quotations embodied in critical articles
or reviews. For information, address St. Martin's Press,
175 Fifth Avenue, New York, N.Y. 10010.

www.minotaurbooks.com

Library of Congress Cataloging-in-Publication Data

Crider, Bill, 1941–
    A knife in the back / Bill Crider.—1st ed.
      p.   cm.
    ISBN 0-312-27184-0
    1. College teachers—Fiction.   2. English teachers—Fiction.   3. Women
teachers—Fiction.   I. Title.

PS3553.R497 K58   2002
813'.54—dc21
                                                                2002069275

First Edition: September 2002

10   9   8   7   6   5   4   3   2   1

To the Kingston Trio
with gratitude for the music
that I've enjoyed for so many years

A KNIFE IN THE BACK

1

Dr. Sally Good sat at her desk, staring at a stack of ungraded freshman essays that lay amid the clutter, and regretting what she was afraid might turn out to be a terrible mistake. She had violated one of her major rules for department chairs: Never date the staff.

Not that she'd actually dated one of the staff yet. But what she'd done was almost as bad. She'd said she'd go out with Jack Neville.

Her feeling of regret was no reflection on Jack. He was a nice-enough guy in his shy, self-effacing way, but ever since becoming head of the English department at Hughes Community College, Sally had deliberately avoided any kind of emotional involvement with the members of the college community.

It wasn't that she hadn't been attracted to some of them. In fact, she had to admit to a slight flutter every now and again when she encountered Jorge "Rooster" Rodriguez. The fact that Jorge was a convicted killer had nothing to do with the flutter, or so she told herself. It was less easy to tell herself that his powerful physique, which she ardently hoped was the result of pumping iron rather than steroid ingestion, had nothing to do with the way he made her feel.

She knew it wasn't the tattoos, which she'd seen in the summer when Jorge wore short-sleeved shirts. His bulging arms were covered with them, and they weren't particularly imaginative. Typical jailhouse fare, Sally told herself: snakes and spiders and skulls and weeping eyes. The rooster was supposedly concealed underneath Jorge's shirts, and Sally hadn't seen it.

For some reason, contemplating Jorge's tattoos caused Sally to breathe a little faster. To take her mind off them, she opened the bottom drawer of her desk and looked for a Hershey bar. Thank God there was one in there. She was reaching for it when someone came into the office.

She sat up, regretting (and not for the first time) her open-door policy. She closed the drawer quickly without grabbing the Hershey bar and turned guiltily toward the door. Anna Trojan was standing there, looking uncertainly at her department chair.

There was nothing unusual in that. Anna Trojan was small and mousey, with gray hair and sallow skin. She always wore gray clothes that were nearly the same shade as her hair, and she looked uncertainly at everyone: students, faculty, and administration. Sally thought that Anna probably looked uncertainly at her own reflection in the mirror.

Anna was the oldest member of the department, though Sally didn't know exactly how old that was. She'd never bothered to look at the personnel records and find out. It had never seemed important.

"What can I do for you, Anna?" Sally said, trying to look like a professional educator instead of someone who'd just been diving for a Hershey bar.

"I think the students are making fun of me," Anna said.

Uncertainly, of course.

Sally straightened in her chair. "I'm sure you're mistaken," she said.

"Well, I could be, of course. Maybe they weren't, after all." Anna turned to go. "I'm sorry I bothered you."

"Wait," Sally said. She hadn't meant to brush Anna off. "Come in and have a seat. Let's talk about this."

Anna turned back to the office. "Well, if you're sure it's no bother."

"No bother at all," Sally said.

She got up and moved a stack of papers from the chair beside her desk. According to Benjamin Franklin's autobiography, the great man had always had trouble keeping things in their proper places. In his vain but commendable attempt to achieve moral perfection, orderliness had given him considerable trouble. Sally took as much comfort as she could from that fact.

"Have a seat," Sally said, putting the papers on an old typing table that was already covered with other papers, a few desk copies of textbooks, and a box of pencils, not to mention an electric typewriter that hadn't been out from under its cover since Sally had moved into the office. She wasn't even sure it still worked, not that it mattered.

Anna sat in the chair and crossed her hands in her lap as she waited for Sally to sit back down.

"Now then," Sally said when she had returned to her place, "what seems to be the trouble?"

"I think the students are making fun of me," Anna repeated. "But I'm probably wrong."

"Maybe," Sally said. "But why do you think so?"

"Well," Anna said, as uncertainly as ever, "this morning there were several students making noise in the hallway while I was teaching my eight o'clock class. They were right outside my door, and I thought at first they'd go away. But they didn't. After a few minutes, I stepped outside and asked them to be quiet."

"And they weren't?" Sally said.

"Oh, no, they got quiet. But just as I was closing my door, I thought I heard one of them say, 'Who was that old lady?' "

"I see," Sally said, though she really didn't. If the worst thing students these days called you was an old lady, you could consider yourself lucky.

"And that's not all," Anna said.

"They called you something else?"

"No. Not them. It was my students. The ones in my class."

"The ones who are making fun of you?"

"They might not be making fun of me. You said so yourself. I could have been mistaken."

Sally repressed a sigh. "Tell me what they said."

"It wasn't what they said so much," Anna told her. "It was the way they said it."

"And how was that?"

"It's my name," Anna said. "They were saying it funny."

"They were calling you 'Anna'?"

"No, they were calling me Ms. Trojan. But there was something about the way they were saying it."

Sally could hardly believe Anna's puzzlement, though it seemed genuine enough. How anyone with the name of Trojan could go through life without having been made aware of its association with a popular brand of condoms was a mystery.

Or maybe I'm just more sophisticated than I give myself credit for, Sally thought.

She was trying to think of a good way to explain things to Anna when Troy Beauchamp, the school gossip, came down the hall and turned straight into the office.

Troy was a sloppy dresser, and today he looked particularly harried. His shirttail bagged out over the top of his pants, and his tie was askew. He came to an abrupt stop when he saw Anna.

"Sorry," he said. "I didn't know anyone was in here."

"I'll be with you in a few minutes, Troy," Sally said. "Would you mind waiting in the hall? And close the door, please."

"I, uh, this is really important news," Troy said.

Everything Troy found out was important, at least to him. He loved being the first to know everything, and he always regarded his latest tidbit as at least as important as the most recent news from Washington, Russia, or the Vatican. He reminded Sally of Emmeline Grangerford, one of the minor characters in *The Adventures of Huckleberry Finn.* Whenever someone died, Emmeline was the first person to arrive at the house after the doctor. Except once. That time the undertaker got there ahead of her, and after that she just pined away. Sally was sure that if anyone ever got to a piece of

4

gossip before Troy, the same thing would happen to him.

"I'm sure your news can wait," Sally told Troy.

"No," Troy said. "It can't. Ralph Bostic has been murdered!"

"What?" Anna said, aghast. She was aghast almost as frequently as she was uncertain. "Isn't he one of the college's trustees?"

"That's right," Troy said, looking at her as if he might be wondering just how many people named *Ralph Bostic* she could possibly know. "And you'll never guess who killed him."

"President Fieldstone?" Sally said.

"Good guess," Troy said approvingly. President Fieldstone's relationship with the board of trustees had been somewhat rocky of late. "But wrong. It's a lot worse than that."

"It couldn't possibly be worse than that," Sally said.

Troy looked somber. "Oh, yes, it could," he said.

Sally didn't know how, but she was sure of one thing: Troy was going to be the first to tell her.

2

—◆—

Jack Neville sat at his office desk, staring at the seventeen-inch screen of his computer monitor. Jack had been in recovery for several days, working on his own little twelve-step program, and he'd finally overcome his addiction to playing Minesweeper on his computer. It hadn't been easy, and he wasn't at all sure how long he could keep himself busy with other things, but so far he'd been able to resist the compelling lure of the game.

There was only one problem: To break himself of the Minesweeper habit, he'd resorted to trying another game, a form of solitaire called Freecell. And now he was in serious danger of becoming addicted to that.

He knew the signs: there was the nearly uncontrollable urge to see the cards fly into place when he made the final correct move, the sweaty desire to see if he could finish the game without once having to pause to think, the powerful craving to experience the thrill of seeing ten moves in advance that everything was going to fall exactly into place. Not to mention the desire to see if he could extend his winning streak, which currently stood at seventy-three games in a row. Not that he was counting.

Jack's hand gripped the computer mouse, and his right index finger trembled as he tried to keep it from double-clicking on the Freecell icon that was so enticingly displayed on the monitor.

Stop it, he told himself. *You know you have other things to do, important departmental business.*

He eased the cursor down to the word-processing icon, and he double-clicked the mouse. The clean white sheet of virtual paper filled the screen, and Jack allowed himself to relax. The crisis was over. For now, at least.

He located the folder where he kept his course syllabi and opened it. Then he opened the file for his American literature course. It had been a couple of years since he'd updated the syllabus, and it was time to revise it and turn it in to Wynona Reed, the academic dean's secretary.

Hughes Community College was going to be visited by its accrediting agency in a few months, and everyone was supposed to have turned in updated syllabi for all classes by the time of the visit. Jack had been putting off the chore for several weeks, since revising a syllabus was roughly as interesting as watching concrete harden, but now he was glad to have something to distract him from Freecell.

Of course there were plenty of other things to distract him if he let them. For one thing, he'd actually gotten up the nerve to ask Sally Good for a date, and she'd surprised him by accepting. In fact, she'd said she'd be glad to go out with him.

But he wasn't sure he believed it. Maybe she'd accepted just so she wouldn't hurt his feelings. Or maybe it was because they'd just been through a pretty harrowing experience, what with the murder of Val Hurley, the art department chair, and all that went along with it.

She was probably already regretting that she'd accepted, he thought. He knew very well the kinds of complications that could arise from dating her, and he knew she must be aware of them as well. In fact, she was probably a lot more aware of them than he was.

There were people who'd say he was dating her only to improve his position in the department, to get a better schedule, and to get more chances to teach the coveted sophomore literature classes. Ellen Baldree would be the first one to say something like that, Jack was certain. She wouldn't say it to Jack, of course, but she'd say it to anyone else who'd listen. And there were plenty of people who'd listen.

Jack tried to concentrate on his syllabus and forget about playing Freecell or dating his department chair, but he found it impossible to be very much concerned about whether to leave Melville out of the syllabus again or whether Poe really deserved three days of classroom time, especially if Melville were eliminated entirely. It didn't seem fair to eliminate Melville, somehow, but Jack didn't really care. He didn't like the selections by Melville in the text, and there was no way his students would read *Moby-Dick*. He might as well ask them to read the entire *Iliad* in ancient Greek.

He made a few minor changes, saved them, and closed the file on the syllabus. Maybe he could focus on something else. He was very interested in the popular culture of the 1950s, and he'd written several articles in the field. The articles hadn't been published in reputable scholarly journals, but no one at Hughes cared about that sort of thing. Teachers at Hughes were supposed to teach, and if they found time to write, well, that was fine. But publications weren't even considered when a person was up for tenure. Student evaluations were a lot more important in the community college scheme of things than published articles.

That was fine with Jack. He could write about things that interested him and publish wherever he wanted to, or wherever he could get something accepted.

He'd been working on an article about the Kingston Trio, the group that had sold millions of albums and started the so-called folk revival in the late 1950s. His thesis was that the Trio's original members, Dave Guard, Bob Shane, and Nick Reynolds, had been far more influential than they had ever received credit for, and that in fact their music and style had had even more significant and long-lasting repercussions in popular music than anything the Beatles had done.

He had a feeling that no one would agree with him, except maybe a few die-hard Kingston Trio fanatics, assuming such people existed, but if he could make his arguments strong and cogent enough, the article might stir up a little controversy. Editors of the kind of publications he submitted his work to liked controversy. It sold magazines, and it usually brought in a lot of letters from readers.

He opened his KT file and started reading. What he'd done so far seemed pretty good to him, and for at least ten minutes he forgot his worries about dating Sally Good. He even managed to forget the Freecell game.

Then there was a knock on his door. He got up and opened it reluctantly. He didn't want to have to spend a half hour explaining to some wayward student why there was no extra-credit work allowed in his classes, why pop quizzes could not be "made up" at a later date, or why term papers written in pencil on both sides of the paper simply weren't acceptable.

As it turned out, he wasn't going to have to do any of those things. Standing outside his office door was Eric Desmond, the chief of Hughes Community College's security services. The head cop. He was nearly sixty, but he didn't look a day over forty, possibly because he was a fitness fanatic. Or maybe he just had good genes. At any rate, Jack knew that Desmond worked out religiously, and he took all kinds of herbal supplements and vitamins. Maybe some of them were working.

"What's up, Chief?" Jack said by way of greeting.

"There's someone here who wants to talk to you," Desmond said, glancing back over his shoulder.

Desmond wasn't alone. Standing behind him was Detective Weems of the local police, with whom Jack had recently become acquainted under what Jack considered thoroughly unpleasant circumstances.

Weems probably wanted to talk about Val Hurley's murder, Jack thought, though all that should have been wrapped up some time ago.

"Come on in," Jack said, moving away from the door to make as much room as he could. His office couldn't be called spacious by any means, but there was space in it for three adults if they didn't mind a little crowding.

Desmond stepped inside, and Weems followed, closing the door behind him. Weems was tall, thick through the waist, and didn't dress nearly as well as Desmond. He clearly didn't place the same premium on fitness that Desmond did, and he probably didn't take herbal supplements, either. The office suddenly seemed much smaller to Jack.

"I'm sorry I can't offer both of you chairs," he said. There was only one chair in the office besides the one behind his desk.

"That's all right," Weems said, looking disdainfully at the stuffed bookshelves on the wall. "We don't mind standing."

"What can I do for you?" Jack said.

Weems smiled unpleasantly, which Jack thought was probably the only way he knew how to smile.

"You can tell me why you killed Ralph Bostic," he said.

3

It's Jack Neville," Troy Beauchamp said. "The fuzz are busting him right now."

Sally was a little too young ever to have heard anyone say "the fuzz are busting him" before, but she knew what Troy meant. And she didn't believe it for a second.

"You're joking," she said.

"No, no. I wouldn't joke about a thing like that," Troy assured her.

"I should hope not," Anna Trojan said. "But I hope you know that 'busting' isn't correct English, Troy. You should say *bursting*. As English teachers, we have to remember that we're role models for our students."

For about a millionth of a second, the image of the police bursting Jack flashed through Sally's mind. It was funny and scary at the same time.

"Where is this supposed to be happening?" she asked.

"Jack's office," Troy said. "I was on my way here to tell you that someone had killed Bostic when I saw the fuzz at Jack's office. My shoelace was flopping on the floor, so I had to stop by the door and tie it. I heard them accuse Jack of killing Bostic."

Sally could easily picture Troy bending over to listen outside the office door. For him, it wouldn't be unusual behavior at all. It was no wonder that he was always first to know things.

"What did the policemen look like?" she asked.

"One of them was Eric Desmond. I didn't know the other one, but I saw him around when Val Hurley was killed."

"Tall?" Sally said. "Stout? Not a happy man?"

"That's the one," Troy said.

"Weems," Sally said. "Good lord. And you're sure Ralph Bostic was murdered?"

"Positive. I heard about it on the radio when I was driving in this morning. He was found at his auto shop, slumped over his desk with a knife sticking out of his back."

"Maybe he didn't fix someone's car correctly," Anna said. "I remember once when I took my car there to get a tune-up. I got a bill for nearly five hundred dollars."

"I don't think anyone would kill him for overcharging," Troy said.

Sally wasn't so sure. She'd heard stories about Bostic's business practices before. But Jack, who wasn't known for being a big spender, would never take his car to someone like Bostic. On the other hand, Jack and Bostic had clashed over other matters involving Bostic's professional life.

"I'd better get down to Jack's office," she said. "I'm his department chair, after all."

"It's too late for Jack," Troy said, shaking his head sadly, as if his colleague had already been tried, convicted, and sent to death row to wait for the gurney that would wheel him into the room to receive his lethal injection. "Once the fuzz get their hands on you, it's all over."

"Not this time," Sally said. "Anna, we'll deal with your students later. I'm sorry, but this situation is something that won't wait."

"I understand," Anna said. "I'm sure that no one wants the fuzz to burst anyone around here."

"Right," Sally said, standing up. She really, really needed a Hershey bar. "Excuse me, Troy."

She brushed past him and went out the office door, not running but hurrying right along. She heard Troy right behind her. She should have known that he wasn't going to miss something like this, not if he could help it. She picked up her pace, and when she turned the corner of the hall, she ran right into Jorge Rodriguez.

Jorge wrapped his arms around her to keep her from falling and held her to him for just a fraction of a second. But in that fraction, Sally realized just how strong Jorge's arms were and how solid his chest was. There were some people, Sally knew, who opposed letting prison inmates have access to fitness equipment, but she wasn't one of them. She could see and feel what that access had done for Jorge, and she definitely approved. At least she did as long as she could believe that Jorge's physique owed everything to hours on the Nautilus machine and nothing to steroid abuse.

"Where are you going in such a hurry?" Jorge asked as he released Sally on her own recognizance.

"Jack's office," Troy Beauchamp said.

He was standing right behind Sally with a look of disapproval on his face. Sally hadn't been at Hughes long before she learned that while quite a few of the women on campus found Jorge dangerously interesting, most of the men tended to avoid him.

Jorge was the campus liaison with the Texas Department of Criminal Justice, Institutional Division. In other words, he worked with the college's prison programs, a job made to order for a former inmate who had rehabilitated himself through education while serving his sentence for murder. No one was quite sure just how the murder had occurred, and it was the subject of any number of rumors, some of which cast Jorge in the role of a practically blameless avenging angel. Others were not nearly so flattering. Sally occasionally wondered what the truth was; at other times, she was convinced that she didn't really want to know.

"What's the problem with Jack?" Jorge asked.

"I'm not sure," Sally said, with a glance back at Troy. "Maybe nothing."

"In other words, it's private departmental business."

"I suppose you could say that."

"Well, then, I'll leave you to it," Jorge said. "If there's anything I can do, let me know."

"I will," Sally said, though she wasn't sure what Jorge could do. On the other hand, if Jack's trouble really did involve murder, Jorge might be just the person to talk to.

"We'd better hurry," Troy said, and Sally moved away from Jorge. She couldn't resist a look back over her shoulder as he turned the corner.

"I wonder where he was when Bostic was killed?" Troy said.

"Do you think he might have done it?"

Troy shrugged. "Well, you know how Bostic felt about the prison program."

Sally knew, though it hadn't occurred to her. Bostic believed that weight-lifting equipment wasn't the only thing inmates shouldn't have access to. He didn't think they should have access to television, air-conditioning, or free medical care. And he especially didn't think they should have access to education. In spite of all the studies that showed education was just about the only effective method of reducing recidivism, Bostic was a zealous and vocal opponent of the college's classes in the prison units.

"If Bostic had his way, Jorge would be out of a job," Troy pointed out.

"So would several of our faculty members," Sally said. "We make quite a bit of money from those prison classes. It's a classic win-win situation: We profit financially, and the prisoners profit from their educations."

"That's not the way Bostic sees it," Troy said. "Or *saw* it, to use the correct verb tense."

Sally remembered some of Bostic's more intemperate comments during his campaign for the college board of trustees. One of them had to do with the fact that instead of helping the greater human community by teaching in the prisons, Hughes was "just helping produce a more educated criminal class that will know more ways of getting away with their crimes."

16

Jorge had been especially proud of the computer classes in the prisons, but Bostic had objected to those more loudly than to any others. He saw them as "just a way to train crooks to steal from you over the Internet. They'll get your credit cards and your Social Security numbers, and the next thing you know they'll *be* you. Either that, or they'll set one of those viruses loose and destroy your financial records."

Nevertheless, Sally didn't think Bostic's opinions, as wrong-headed as they were, could have been a reason for Jorge to kill someone, and she said as much to Troy.

"Well," Troy said, "he's done it before."

Sally didn't have a comeback for that. She knocked on the door of Jack's office, but there was no answer. She knocked again, and then used her pass key. The door swung open, but there was no one inside.

4

Jack was familiar with the phrase *taken in for questioning* only from television and the movies, but he wasn't surprised to learn that in real life, things went pretty much as they did on screen.

He was escorted outside the classroom building and put into an unmarked car. All he could think of at the time was how glad he was that classes were going on, so both the hall outside his office and the parking lot were practically deserted. It was bad enough that Chief Desmond had to see his humiliation. At least there were no students to witness it.

He hadn't been handcuffed. That was another thing to be grateful for. Maybe that meant that Weems didn't think he was dangerous, which of course he wasn't. Sure, he'd killed a roach or two, and once he'd run over a turtle that was trying to cross a freeway, but he'd done it only because there was a car right beside him that prevented him from swerving aside. He'd felt terrible about it for days afterward. And he didn't even especially like turtles.

He hadn't especially liked Ralph Bostic, either. Everyone knew that Bostic was a crook, or at least a cheat, notorious for overcharging anyone who made the mistake of taking an automobile to his shop for repair. Jack disliked Bostic for similar reasons, all right, but maybe Weems wouldn't ask him about those.

Or maybe he would. Jack made no attempt to engage the detective in conversation as they drove to the police station, and

Weems didn't seem inclined to talk. The silence grew heavy, and Jack started feeling guilty, which he figured was exactly the way Weems had planned things. Knowing that, however, didn't help matters. Jack began to recall all his many sins, while trying to balance them with his few virtues.

There was the turtle, of course, accident or not. And there was the time he'd sneaked into the movie theater without paying when a friend opened the exit door and let him inside. He knew he'd made more than one rolling stop in his time, and he exceeded the speed limit nearly every time he got on the highway, even though he told himself that he did so merely to keep from being run over and flattened by the eighteen-wheelers that were exceeding it more than he was. As far as he could remember, he'd never stolen anything, though he might have taken a comic book from a grocery store rack when he was a kid. He just wasn't sure. But if he had, it had happened only once. He'd never sexually harassed his female students, or the male ones, either, for that matter, and he'd always graded them strictly on the merits of their work rather than allowing any personal prejudices to interfere. And he'd certainly never killed anyone.

Not that Weems would believe that.

The detective continued to ignore him as he drove the car around to the back of the building that housed the town's new police station and jail. Jack had never even thought about the police station as having a rear entrance, but he had a feeling he was going to learn a lot more about the place than he wanted to know.

They got out of the car and Weems led Jack inside the building. As they walked through an echoing hallway, a man dressed in an orange jumpsuit stepped aside to let them pass. Jack knew the man must be a prisoner, a trusty who was allowed a little freedom because of his good behavior. Or at least Jack hoped that's what he was, and not some crazed escapee. Weems nodded to the man and seemed to know him, and Jack considered that a good sign.

He didn't consider it a good sign, however, when Weems

opened a door and said, "Here's the interview room. Just step inside, please."

The room was even more uncomfortable than an adjunct instructor's office. It was furnished with a little wooden table and a couple of beat-up folding chairs. Jack wondered why they hadn't bought new furniture when they'd built the jail. Or maybe they had. Maybe it just suffered from hard use.

"Have a seat," Weems told him.

Jack sat at the table in the less rickety-looking of the two chairs. There was a little metal ashtray on the table. Jack noted that it was far too small for use as a weapon.

"Smoke if you want to," Weems said.

"I don't smoke," Jack said, trying to relax in the chair, which wasn't easy. Every time he moved, even a little bit, the chair gave out with a metallic squeal.

Weems leaned up against the wall, looking as casual as if he questioned murder suspects every day. There was a thick mirrored glass set into the wall beside him. Jack knew it wasn't a mirror from the other side.

Weems saw where Jack was looking and nodded at the glass.

"That's right," he said. "It's a two-way mirror. There's somebody watching from the other side, and everything you say is being recorded. But you knew that already."

Actually, Jack hadn't known about the recording, and he wasn't sure he believed it even now, but he didn't say anything.

"Everybody thinks they know every damn thing these days," Weems went on. Jack didn't bother to correct his error in pronoun-antecedent agreement. "It's television. They watch some idiotic cop show like *Nash Bridges*, and they think that's the way things really work."

"They don't?" Jack said.

Weems looked at him with thinly disguised contempt.

"Of course they don't."

Jack didn't really care, so he sat there, looking at the mirror and wondering who was behind it. After a while he said, "Aren't you going to read me my rights?"

"See?" Weems said. "Television."

"You don't have to read me my rights?"

"Not if we're just having a little friendly conversation here. And that's what we're having, right?"

"Sure," Jack said, without enthusiasm, looking at the mirror. "Who's going to be the good cop?"

"That's a joke, right? Because of what I said about TV? But it's not as funny as you think. See, this is such a small town that we can't afford a good cop and a bad cop for questioning a suspect. I have to be the good cop and bad cop both."

"I'll write a letter to my city councilperson about increasing police salaries."

"That's a fine idea. I could use the extra money. But it won't do you any good to try sucking up to me. So tell me, why did you kill Ralph Bostic?"

"I didn't kill anybody," Jack said. He put his forearms on the table and leaned forward. There were several spots that looked like blood near the ashtray, but Jack thought they might be ketchup. He hoped they were, at any rate. "I told you at the school. I didn't even know Bostic was dead. I still don't."

"It's been on the radio," Weems said. "If it's been on the radio, he must be dead. The news media doesn't make mistakes like that."

"Look," Jack said, refraining from telling Weems that *media* required a plural verb, "I'm a law-abiding guy. I was a big help to you the last time you had a murder case, remember. I *like* the police."

That wasn't strictly true, but it seemed like the right thing to say. It also wasn't strictly true that Jack had been a big help to Weems. Sally Good deserved most of the credit, if not all of it. But Jack thought he might work his way into Weems's good graces by reminding him of the Val Hurley case.

It didn't work.

"You were more of a hindrance than anything," Weems said. "If you and Sally Good had stayed out of my way, I'd have arrested the killer a lot sooner."

Wow, Jack thought. *Talk about not strictly true!* Left alone, Weems would probably have arrested the wrong person, and even that would have taken him months.

"What makes you think I killed Bostic, anyway?" Jack asked. "I haven't even seen him in weeks."

"You sure about that?"

"Of course I'm sure."

"You didn't see him any more recently than that? Like last night?"

"No, I didn't see him last night. Is that when he was killed?"

"You should know."

Jack took a deep breath and leaned back. The chair squealed, and Jack thought it was going to fall over. He grabbed at the seat to steady himself.

Weems watched impassively, but Jack was sure he was laughing on the inside. The flimsy chair was all part of the set-up, like the ketchup stains and the one-way glass, all of it designed to make Jack feel uncomfortable and guilty. Well, it wasn't working. He'd felt guilty in the car, but now he was just feeling angry.

"Why won't you answer my questions?" he asked. "I have a right to know what's going on here."

"You're being questioned," Weems said. "About the murder of Ralph Bostic. You say you're not guilty. I think you are. That's about the size of it."

"Why do you think I'm guilty?"

"Where were you last night?"

Jack sighed. It was clear that he wasn't going to get any real answers unless he did some talking of his own, so he decided to cooperate. To a certain extent.

"What time?" he asked.

"Let's say between nine and ten o'clock."

"All right. Let's say that. Between nine and ten o'clock last night, I was at home."

"Alone?"

"That's right. Home alone. Sounds like a good title for a movie, doesn't it."

"Movie?"

"Never mind," Jack said.

Jack liked movies, but Weems probably hadn't been to one since he was a kid and his mother dumped him off at the mall theater while she went shopping for Christmas gifts.

"So you were watching a movie?" Weems said.

"No," Jack told him. "I was reading a book."

"Was it *Beowulf* by any chance?"

"Huh?"

"*Beowulf.* You've heard of it, right?"

"Sure. I was just surprised to hear you mention it."

"I'm not just some uneducated jerk, you know," Weems said. "People think that about cops, but it's not true. There's this new translation of *Beowulf* that I was reading last week. It's pretty good."

"I've read it," Jack said. If Weems was being the good cop now, Jack was willing to play along. "And I agree. But I wasn't reading it last night. I was reading a biography of Walt Whitman."

"Never cared for him," Weems said. "I don't much like free verse. So that's it? That's your alibi? You were at home reading a book about Walt Whitman?"

Jack could just imagine how an alibi like that would be regarded by a tough prosecutor. Or even a namby-pamby one, if there was such a thing.

"That's it," he said.

"Then things don't look too good for you," Weems said.

"Why not? What in the world makes you think I killed Ralph Bostic?"

"Because you didn't like him."

Well, that was true. Jack couldn't very well deny it. But he wondered how Weems knew it.

"Everybody knows about it," Weems said, as if reading Jack's mind.

Jack thought it was just another cop trick, like the chair and the mirror and the stains. But if it was, it was a pretty good one.

"It was even in the paper," Weems said. "You had a big argument at the last meeting of the college board of trustees, even got into a little yelling match."

Jack had been hoping Weems didn't know about the yelling. But he couldn't deny it. Not entirely.

"I wasn't doing any yelling," he said.

Weems shrugged. "Maybe so, maybe not, but Bostic was. Nearly had a stroke, the way I heard it."

"It wasn't quite that bad," Jack said.

"Yeah, well, if somebody had accused me of being a crook in front of everybody, including a reporter from the local rag, I might even have a stroke myself."

Jack didn't believe that for a minute. He was pretty sure that nothing bothered Weems that much.

"I didn't exactly accuse him of being a crook," he said.

"Sure you did. You said he had a big conflict of interest, that he was gouging the college for money, and that he should resign from the board. But he didn't resign, so you got rid of him another way. By killing him."

"You keep saying that, but I don't think you have any proof," Jack said. "Otherwise we wouldn't be having this friendly conversation, as you called it. You'd have arrested me and locked me up."

"I have the proof," Weems assured him. "It would just make things easier if you'd admit it."

"Well, I'm not," Jack said. "Mainly because I didn't do it."

Weems shook his head sadly.

"I miss the old days," he said. "If this was the old days, I could get out the rubber hose and beat the truth out of you."

Jack couldn't tell for sure, but he thought Weems might be joking. He hoped so.

"But if you don't want to confess, that's okay," Weems went on. "Like I said, I have the proof."

"You still haven't mentioned just what that might be, though."

"Your knife," Weems said.

"My knife?"

"Yeah, your knife. The one that has your initials on the blade. The one you left sticking in Ralph Bostic's back."

Damn, Jack thought. *I knew I never should have signed up for that knife-making class.*

5

The bell rang while Sally was standing there looking into Jack Neville's deserted office, and students poured out of the classrooms to fill the hallway, some laughing, some talking, some pulling out their cell phones. Some were heading for the vending machines, and some were just trying to get outside where they could light a cigarette. Not a one of them paid any attention to Sally and Troy.

"They've hauled him off to the hoosegow," Troy said, sounding to Sally like an actor in an old Roy Rogers movie, and she briefly imagined Jack dressed as a rhinestone cowboy, astride a horse, his hands tied behind him with a piece of a dirty lariat.

Sally almost smiled, but she realized it was a time for serious action, not fantasy. She turned and left the office, pulled the door shut behind her, and brushed past Troy.

"Where are you going?" he asked.

"To get Jack. He has a class in room one-fifty-nine next hour. Go dismiss his students before you go to your own class, please."

"I'll write a note on the board," Troy said. "That way I can go with you."

"I don't need any help. Just dismiss the class."

Sally made her way back to her office through a crowd of swarming students. She picked up her purse and turned off her light. Just before she shut the door, she went back inside and got a Hershey bar out of the desk drawer. If she ever needed a quick pick-me-up, she needed it now.

She munched on the candy bar as she walked toward the rooms that housed the campus police station. As much as she liked chocolate, she could hardly taste it for worrying about Jack.

She finished the Hershey in time to toss the paper into the trash can in front of the cop shop. She went inside and asked the dispatcher, a chunky blond civilian, for Chief Desmond.

Desmond stepped out of his office before the dispatcher could call him. He said, "If you're here about Jack, you don't have anything to worry about. He'll be fine."

"How do you know that?" Sally asked.

Desmond ushered her into his office, closed the door, and offered her a chair. Sally said she preferred to stand.

"Jack's just been taken in for questioning," Desmond said. "I'm sure the police don't really suspect him."

"That's not the way I heard it."

"How did the word get out so fast?"

"Troy Beauchamp."

"I should have known. Does anything ever happen that he doesn't know about?"

"Probably not. What I want to know is whether I need bail money for Jack."

Desmond smiled. "Of course not. He hasn't been arrested. I told you: It's not serious."

"It's serious to me. I'm going to get him out."

"He's probably out already if he cooperated. I'm sure he's not a serious suspect."

"Who is, then?"

"Weems didn't tell me."

"I didn't think he would." Sally opened the door. "I'm going to see if I can help Jack."

Desmond shrugged. "If you want to, go ahead. But you're probably wasting your time."

"I'll take the risk," Sally said.

28

She was getting into her Acura Integra when Troy Beauchamp came running up.

"I'm going with you," he said. "I'm Jack's friend, too, and he needs all the friends he can get right now."

"What about the classes?"

"I got Wynona to dismiss them."

"You didn't tell her why, did you?" Sally asked.

"Of course not," Troy said, settling into the passenger seat. "I know better than that. Wynona's quite a gossip, you know."

Wynona Reed had big hair, big eyes, and a big mouth. Unlike Troy, she wasn't the first to find things out, but she always found out eventually. Her intelligence system might not work fast, but it was second to none. She had been at Hughes for more than twenty years and remembered everything that had happened during that time. Everything. If there was a skeleton in a closet, Wynona could rattle it. If there was a buried secret, Wynona could, if she chose to, hand you a shovel and tell you where to dig. If there was an embarrassing incident that every other person on campus had forgotten about, Wynona probably had it recorded on videotape. And she was not exactly the soul of discretion.

Sally started the car and headed out of the lot.

"Luckily there aren't any other gossips at the college," she said, looking at Troy out of the corner of her eye.

"I'm hurt," he said, catching the look. "You know I'd never say anything that might reflect badly on anybody."

"I just wanted to be sure," Sally said as she turned onto the street and headed for the police station.

"You admit it was your knife, then?" Weems said.

"No. I admit that I made one in a class I took," Jack said. "But someone stole it. I kept it in my office, and I never lock the door. It disappeared weeks ago."

Weems sighed. "Let me ask you a question," he said.

"Isn't that what you've been doing?"

"I mean another kind of question. How many times have you had students tell you that they couldn't turn in a paper because their grandfather had died?"

Jack could already see where Weems was going, but he answered anyway.

"Lots of times. I don't keep a count. I do sometimes tell the students at the beginning of the semester that they might want to drop my class and take another one if their relatives aren't in good health because there's a pretty high mortality rate among the grandparents of my students."

"They don't get the joke, though, do they?"

"No."

"And when they come in to tell you their grandfather has died they think it's a really clever, original excuse, one that nobody ever thought of before, right?"

"Probably," Jack said.

"But it's not. Students have been using it ever since I was in college and a long time before that, I'll bet. It's something every teacher has heard a hundred times."

Jack just nodded.

"Well," Weems said, "that's the way it is with the old 'somebody stole it' story. Every time we arrest some guy whose car's been used in a robbery, he tells us that the car was stolen an hour before the crime was committed. Whenever we find a gun at a crime scene and trace it to some guy with a rap sheet longer than *War and Peace*, he tells us that the gun was stolen months before we found it. You see what I'm getting at?"

"I'm way ahead of you," Jack told him.

"Good. Then you can see that your excuse isn't very original. I'm a little disappointed in you. I thought you could come up with a better one."

"I didn't know I was going to need one," Jack said. "How about this one: My fingerprints aren't on the knife."

"How do you know that? Because you wiped them off?"

"No. Because if they were, you'd have booked me already. My

30

prints are on file because I've taught classes at the prison units, and you'd have checked them immediately. If you'd gotten a match, I'd be in a cell right now. So you might as well admit it. You don't really have any evidence. Well, you might have my knife, but you can't prove I used it."

"You don't have an alibi," Weems pointed out.

"I don't need one if you can't prove I was at Bostic's place when he was killed."

"We'll see about that."

"We certainly will. Which reminds me. Now I remember something else that I learned on TV."

"What's that?" Weems said. "You've just remembered that you'd better call your lawyer?"

Jack shook his head. "That's not it. I didn't think I'd need a lawyer when you brought me here, and I still don't think so."

"What is it, then?"

"I think I'll leave now."

"What makes you think you can do that?"

"I think I can do it because this is just a friendly question-and-answer session. It's not like I'm under arrest or anything."

"You probably watch *Law and Order*," Weems said. "I'll bet that's where you learned that."

"It doesn't matter where," Jack said. "What matters is whether I'm right."

"You're right," Weems said. "But let me tell you something."

Jack felt himself relaxing all over. Now that he had the upper hand, he was getting almost comfortable in the squeaky metal chair. A college English teacher could outsmart a cop any day of the week, even a cop who read *Beowulf*.

"Sure," Jack said. "Tell me."

"I'm going to be watching you like a hawk," Weems said. His tone, which had been merely unfriendly, turned downright ugly. "I think you killed Bostic, and I'm going to know your every move from now on. When you slip away to that private men's room they have at the college for teachers, I'll know it. When you—"

"We don't have a private men's room," Jack said. "We use the same one the students use. Well, the dean has one in the back of his office, but nobody else ever uses it. Not that I know of, that is."

"Don't try to get me off the track," Weems said. "I'm going to be on you like—"

"White on rice? A cheap suit? Fresh paint on an old barn?"

"All right," Weems said. "That's it. I should've known you'd turn out to be a smart-ass when you thought you were off the hook. But you're not off the hook. Don't ever think that."

"Don't worry," Jack said, standing up. "I won't. Can I go now?"

"It's *may*," Weems said, without the hint of a smile. "You're supposed to say, '*May* I go now.' I'd think an English teacher would know that."

Jack got up and opened the door. Weems made no move to stop him, so Jack went out into the hall. He had the uncomfortable feeling that Weems might still have the upper hand after all.

6

Jack wandered down the hallway toward what he thought might be the front of the building and eventually wound up in an area of offices. He didn't want to ask anyone any questions, so he looked around until he found an unmarked door. He pushed it open and stepped into the main entrance to the police station and jail. The first person he saw was Sally Good, who was standing at a window talking to a uniformed officer behind the glass. Troy Beauchamp stood beside her.

Sally looked around and saw Jack, said something else to the officer, and walked over to where Jack was standing. Troy trailed along behind her.

"Hey," Jack said.

"Hey, yourself, Dillinger," Troy said. "You don't look any the worse for wear."

"Weems didn't give me the full treatment," Jack said. "I think he wanted to, though. It's good to see the two of you. I appreciate your coming down here. I was wondering how I'd get back to campus."

"Your class was dismissed," Sally said. "Are you sure you want to go back to school? I could take you to your house."

"I'll go back. I have another class, and I wouldn't want Weems to think I was scared of him. Let's get out of here."

They went out through the tall glass doors at the front of the building and got into Sally's Integra. Troy thoughtfully sat in the back, which wasn't easy to get into.

"Did you convince them you were innocent?" he asked.

"No," Jack said, and told them the whole story, knowing that Troy would spread it over the campus within ten minutes of his arrival there.

"It sounds as if you're in real trouble," Troy said when Jack was done. "Too bad about that knife. You really should lock your office, you know. We got a memo from Chief Desmond about that not long ago, right after A. B. D. Johnson had those checks stolen. Boy, was he upset."

"He thought it was part of an administrative plot," Sally said. "When he found out that a student had taken them, he felt better about it."

Perry Johnson, better known as A. B. D. because he had finished his graduate work All But the Dissertation, was easily agitated. He saw nearly everything that happened at Hughes as an administrative plot, and everyone suspected that he was on daily, if not hourly, medication to control his blood pressure, which by the end of the day was usually off the chart if the redness of his face was any clue.

"Isn't Perry the one who was really behind that argument you had with Bostic at the board meeting?" Sally asked Jack.

"Yes," Jack said. "He's the one, all right. I wish I'd never gotten involved with that faculty senate."

"We need a group to speak for us," Troy said.

"Sure," Jack agreed. "But I'm not sure that was any of our business."

"It's our business if the school's getting ripped off," Troy said. "We're taxpayers as well as employees."

He had a point, Sally thought, but she suspected that Jack felt pretty much as she did, that the attack on Bostic had been motivated as much by politics as by a desire to protect the district's taxpayers. It was true that Bostic was a crook. He'd received a contract to do the repair work and upkeep on all the school-owned vehicles, and he'd been charging exorbitant rates for the work.

34

Someone had brought this to the attention of the faculty senate and pointed out that not only was the college losing money but there was an enormous conflict of interest now that Bostic was sitting on the board.

She wondered whether the faculty senate would have launched an attack against a more popular board member, one who spoke up for the faculty and who wasn't out to shut down some of the school's programs, even if he was a crook. But maybe she was being too cynical.

On the other hand, maybe she wasn't.

"What got Perry so upset in the first place?" she asked.

"Crooked business dealings," Troy said.

"That's not what I mean. He wouldn't have complained to the faculty senate unless someone had told him what was going on. How did he find out about the business relationship in the first place?"

No one had an answer for that, and as Sally drove on beneath the branches of the oak trees that spread across the streets, she wondered who'd been talking to A. B. D.

When they got back to the school, they went to their offices. Sally waited for a few minutes, then went looking for Jack. He was sitting at his desk, playing Freecell.

She said, "Relaxing, I see."

Jack looked up guiltily.

"I don't blame you," Sally said. She closed the office door. "We need to talk."

She sat in the chair provided for student visitors, and Jack minimized the Freecell screen.

"I've been thinking," Sally began.

"Me, too," Jack said.

"You know that Fieldstone will go ballistic when he hears about this, don't you?"

"I don't blame him. There's no way to make murder look good. It's bad for the college's image."

Sally nodded. It wasn't that Fieldstone wouldn't feel sympathy for the dead man and his family. It was just that one of his main concerns was the school's public image. He was content when the board was content. He liked happy taxpayers. He hated complaints. So did the board members. Sally understood; she didn't like complaints, either. But she didn't think Jack had quite figured out what she was trying to say. Either that, or he was in denial about the position he was in, through no fault of his own.

"Fieldstone's not going to like the idea of having a murder suspect in the classroom," she said.

Jack started to say something, then stopped.

"The students probably wouldn't mind," Sally said. "They know you, and they'll know you couldn't kill anyone. But their parents are a different story. You can imagine the kinds of calls that Fieldstone will be getting. He may be getting them already."

"Are you saying I should stop teaching? Resign?"

"Of course not. I'm not even suggesting a leave of absence. I'm just warning you. You have to be ready if Fieldstone calls you."

"I'll be ready. I guess. I just wish I had more confidence in the police."

"That's one thing you don't have to worry about," Sally said. "I'm sure they'll catch whoever killed Bostic. There must be plenty of people who have motives."

"All his customers, for example," Jack said. "But to catch someone, the police would have to be looking. I don't think that's going to happen."

"Isn't that their job?"

"Sure it is. But Weems made it clear to me who his number-one suspect was. In fact, I don't think he has any other suspects, and I'd be willing to bet he won't be looking for any. I think he's already made up his mind about the killer. He's convinced I'm the guy."

"That's bad."

"What's worse is that I don't think he was joking. I'm not sure he even knows how to joke."

"You have to admit that you're in a pretty bad position. What-ever possessed you to take a knife-making class in the first place?"

Jack thought about it for a couple of seconds.

"It seemed like a good idea at the time."

Sally smiled. "At least *you* can joke about it, but I'm not so sure that's a good idea. This isn't a joking matter."

Jack tried a smile that didn't quite come off.

"What about our date?" he asked. "Are you afraid of being seen with a murder suspect?"

"Not in the least," Sally said, meaning it. That wasn't what worried her about dating Jack.

The telephone on Jack's desk rang, and he answered it.

"Please hold for Dr. Fieldstone," said Eva Dillon, Fieldstone's secretary.

Jack looked at Sally and mouthed the words, "It's the pres."

Sally nodded. Fieldstone would have been getting some of those phone calls, and he'd be summoning Jack to his office. She listened to Jack's side of the conversation, and when he'd finished talking, she said, "So?"

"So, Fieldstone wants me to pay him a little visit."

"I was afraid of that."

"So was I."

"I'll go along," Sally said. "After all, I'm your department chair."

"I don't think that would be a good idea," Jack told her. "It might give him the idea that I'm afraid of him."

"Well, aren't you?"

"Not really. I've just been questioned by the cops. Why should I be afraid of a college president?"

"Because the cops can just put you in prison. Dr. Fieldstone can take away your job."

"I guess I'll just have to convince him that I'm innocent," Jack said.

"How are you going to do that?"

"I don't know," Jack said.

7

Sally went back to her office and sat down at her desk. She resisted the urge to have another Hershey bar, but it wasn't easy. She tried to busy herself with grading a set of multiple-choice quizzes that she'd given her American literature class on one of the reading assignments, but she couldn't stop thinking about Jack and his situation.

One thing she wondered about was the knife that had been used to kill Bostic. Jack's knife. What did that mean? Did someone steal the knife for the purpose of framing Jack? Or did someone steal it and only later decide to use it for the murder? If someone was trying to frame Jack, why?

She couldn't come up with answers any better than those her students had circled on the reading quiz. Several of them thought that "The Short Happy Life of Francis Macomber" was set in New York City. A couple of them thought that Macomber had been shot by "a Mafia hitman." Sally wondered if she was making the choices too difficult, but decided that wasn't the problem. The problem was that some people just hadn't studied the assignment.

Maybe what she needed to do was study the murder more carefully. Maybe then she could discover some answers. For example, she might be able to find out who had clued A. B. D. Johnson in about Bostic's dealings with the college. Sally was sure he couldn't have discovered anything on his own.

It wouldn't do to go directly to A. B. D., of course. He would be sure that she was involved in some plot against him, mainly because he was constantly suspicious of everything and everyone. He believed that the administration was secretly (or not so secretly) conspiring against him and that his fellow faculty members were out to discover the secret topic of his unfinished doctoral dissertation so that they could claim it for their own. While his mild paranoia didn't go a long way toward endearing him to anyone, it would have made him an ideal candidate to pass along information to the board. He would have seen the revelation of Bostic's questionable dealings with the college as a way of striking back at everyone involved.

Sally knew that if she questioned him, he might think that she was somehow trying to undermine his credibility—not that he had any to undermine—or even to get him fired. Sally would have to find out who his source was from someone else. Fortunately, there was someone else who would probably know.

Sally looked out her door toward the office suite of James Naylor, the academic dean, located inconveniently nearby. Sometimes Sally was sure that the dean had assigned her to an office near his own so that he could watch every move she made. In her heart of hearts, she realized that wasn't the case, but anyone who worked in academia at any level had a little bit of A. B. D. Johnson lurking somewhere inside.

Sally saw that Wynona Reed was sitting at her desk in Naylor's outer office, working at the computer. Sally couldn't actually see Wynona because of the computer terminal, but she could see the top of Wynona's copper-colored hair, teased to a majestic height, of which several inches were visible over the top of the monitor.

Sally got up and walked over to the dean's office. She stood quietly in the doorway until Wynona finished whatever she'd been working on and looked up.

Wynona had, besides her brassy, teased hair, a number of outstanding features, including her eyes. It was as if she had bought a book called *Makeup Secrets of TV Evangelists' Wives Revealed!* and made each secret her own.

"You need to see the dean?" Wynona asked. "Because if you do, he's not in there. He's in some kind of meeting with the president and one of your faculty members. I guess you know why."

"I know," Sally said. "Do you?"

Wynona looked smug. "Dr. Naylor tells me pretty much everything."

Sally wasn't sure that was such a good idea, but she, along with everyone else on campus, knew that Naylor was one of Wynona's many sources of information. In Sally's opinion, Wynona knew far too much about the college's business, but there wasn't much Sally could do about it.

"Actually," Sally said, "I didn't come to see the dean. I came to see you."

Wynona didn't pretend to be flattered. Instead, she was suspicious and defensive, which Sally knew was generally the case. She seemed to assume that everyone wanted either to give her more work to do or complain about something she'd done. The truth was that Wynona was good at her job, and hardly anyone ever complained. And while people were always giving her work, it was nothing that wasn't part of her regular duties. Sally thought that Wynona shouldn't complain about doing anything that was just part of her job, but Wynona had a high opinion of her own importance. In fact, it sometimes appeared to Sally that Wynona thought she was actually the dean and Naylor was just some guy who had the big office in back of her.

"I dismissed those classes for you," Wynona said. "If that's what you're worried about."

"I know you did, and I really appreciate it," Sally said. She wasn't too proud to stoop to flattery if it would help.

"Why else would you want to see me?" Wynona asked.

"I thought you might be able to help me out with something," Sally said.

Wynona rolled her big eyes, looking like a raccoon in distress. Then she sighed, as if to indicate that she'd known all along Sally was there just to pile more work in her already overflowing in-box.

"What is it, then?" she asked. "You need some changes in the schedule for next semester? In the book orders? If it's the book orders, you're too late. I've already sent them on to the bookstore."

"It's nothing like that. I was looking for some information."

Immediately Wynona's attitude changed. She smiled and wiggled a bit to get more comfortable in her chair.

"What kind of information?"

"It's something about Ralph Bostic."

"He's dead," Wynona said. "Everybody knows that."

"True," Sally agreed. "But not everybody knows how A. B. D. Johnson got that information he gave the board about Bostic's sweetheart deal with the college."

Wynona's smile widened. "They sure don't."

"But I'll bet you do," Sally said.

"I might. But it's just a rumor. You know I don't like to repeat rumors."

On the contrary, Sally knew that Wynona loved to repeat rumors, but she never liked to do so unless she was getting something in return—something like another rumor.

"I don't like to repeat gossip, either," Sally said. "But did Troy tell you why you were dismissing the classes?"

Wynona looked peeved. "No. I asked him, but he said he was in a hurry."

"He was," Sally said, glad that Wynona didn't accumulate information as quickly as Troy. "We had to get Jack Neville out of jail."

Wynona's mouth got round. Her exaggerated eyes got even larger.

"You're kidding," she said.

"Nope," Sally said, and gave her the short version of the story.

"I can't believe it," Wynona said. "I mean, I knew Ralph Bostic was dead. I can believe that part. I heard it on the radio. What I can't believe is that Jack Neville was arrested."

"Believe it. Now you can see why I'm interested in who gave A. B. D. that information."

"I certainly can. Of course I don't know for sure, but I heard it was Roy Don Talon."

Roy Don Talon had given Sally trouble before. He was a well-known local car salesman whose slogan was DRIVE TO HUGHES FOR HUGE SAVINGS." Apparently a great many people in Houston and other nearby towns took his advice because Talon had made tons of money. He collected cowboy art, and every year he was one of the high bidders for some prize-winning animal at the Houston stock show and rodeo. He cultivated a rhinestone cowboy image in his dress and always wore a big western hat and boots, along with an assortment of jackets that wouldn't have looked out of place on one of the stars of the Grand Ole Opry. Sally suspected that Talon had never been on a horse in his life and had never come any closer to an actual cow than the ones he bid on at the stock show.

She could easily see why Talon wouldn't want Bostic to be ripping off the college by overcharging for vehicle repair. Talon probably thought that if anybody was going to rip off the school, he should be that person. But it wouldn't have been politic for him to turn Bostic in. People would undoubtedly have suspected his motives. For some reason, nobody trusted a car salesman.

"Thanks, Wynona," Sally said. "I appreciate the help."

"Any time," Wynona said, which Sally knew really meant *anytime you have some gossip for me, I'll be glad to trade.* "You're not going to get mixed up in this mess, are you?"

"Who, me?" Sally shook her head. "I know better than to do that again."

Wynona blinked her striking eyes and said, "Sure you do."

8

Jack walked slowly over to Fieldstone's office, and though it was a nice day, he didn't really notice the sunshine or the green grass or the students who passed by him. Some of them waved and said "hi," and Jack always managed to respond. But his mind was on other things.

Like job security. He'd never done anything except teach, not unless you counted the jobs he'd done during the summers of his high school and college years. Those jobs had been okay at the time, but he didn't really think he could go back to washing dishes at a boardinghouse or bagging groceries. He wasn't even sure there were such things as boardinghouses these days. There certainly weren't any around the Hughes campus. Besides, he'd gotten a terrible case of dishpan hands, even though he'd used rubber gloves. His skin had turned red, dried out, and cracked. He wouldn't want to have to deal with that again.

He wondered what sort of work he'd have to do if he went to prison. Whatever it was, it was likely to be worse than washing dishes.

He remembered some of the men he'd taught in classes at the prison units. He wondered if any of the ones who'd failed his classes were still there, and he thought about what kind of revenge they might wreak on him if he wound up imprisoned with them. Getting killed would be the least of his worries. There were worse things: dismemberment, gang rape, maiming. It really didn't do to think about it. *And after all,* he told himself, *no innocent man ever goes to prison.*

"What's so funny, Mr. Neville?" a passing student asked.

"Oh," Jack said. He hadn't even realized that he'd laughed aloud. "I was just thinking."

"Must've been a pretty funny thought."

"Not exactly," Jack said.

Eva Dillon rose from her chair when Jack entered the president's office and smiled at him. It reminded Jack of one of those strained smiles you see on people who are about to deliver some particularly nasty piece of news and hope the smile will somehow help. It hardly ever did.

"Dr. Fieldstone is waiting, Mr. Neville," Eva said. "You can go right in."

Jack went through the heavy wooden door, and Eva pulled it silently shut behind him. Dean Naylor was sitting on the couch, and Fieldstone was behind his massive and entirely clean desk.

Naylor stood up and walked over to Jack, throwing an arm around his shoulders. There was nothing unusual in that. Naylor was a touchy-feely guy, a hugger, in a world when hugging could be dangerous. Sometimes Jack wondered how he had lasted as long as he had without having some kind of sexual harassment complaint lodged against him. He'd probably never hugged Vera Vaughn, the campus's militant feminist. She would have flattened him.

"How are you, Jack?" Naylor asked. "I hope you didn't have any problems with the police."

"Not really," Jack said. "I'm an innocent man."

"Thank God for that," Fieldstone said as Naylor guided Jack toward a seat on the couch.

Fieldstone was immaculate, as always, dressed in an expensive navy blue suit and sparkling white shirt. His tie had probably cost more than Jack's entire outfit, which was composed of khakis and a shirt he'd bought at Wal-Mart. Fieldstone always looked exactly the way a college president should look; confident that he was in control. He walked around his desk to shake hands with Jack before Jack was seated. Then he put the desk between them once again.

Good fences make good neighbors, Jack thought. Or maybe he's just afraid of me. Mad-dog Neville, the psycho killer.

"I'm not at all sure your situation is as amusing as you seem to think it is," Fieldstone said.

"Sorry," Jack said. "I seem to find myself laughing out loud for no reason at all."

Fieldstone looked alarmed.

"Oh, don't worry," Jack said. "I'm not going crazy. At least I don't think I am."

"You could have fooled me," Fieldstone said, trying for a light touch, something that he could seldom manage. "If I were you, I'd be feeling pretty somber right about now."

"I am," Jack said, repressing a smile. "That's probably why I'm laughing. Defense mechanism."

Fieldstone appeared to think the idea over and decide that it was as good an excuse as any. He gave Jack a straight look and said, "The question is, are you guilty?"

"As I said, I'm an innocent man. The police didn't hold me, so I must not be guilty."

"You see?" Fieldstone said. "That's what I mean. You're taking this much too lightly."

"I don't mean to. I just can't see how anyone could believe I'm a killer. Do I look like a murderer to you?"

"No," Fieldstone admitted. "But then most of the people I see on the television news shows don't, either. And some of them have done some terrible things."

He had a point there, Jack conceded, thinking again about the men he'd taught in prison. For the most part, they looked just like everyone else. Nobody passing one of them on the street would ever give him a second glance.

"It doesn't matter how I look," Jack said. "I didn't do it. I'm not capable of something like that."

"I didn't really think you were. But we have to consider the school's position in this."

Here it comes, Jack thought.

"What *is* the school's position?" he asked, maybe a little more sharply than he'd intended.

"Now, Jack," Naylor said from his place beside him on the couch, "there's no need to be upset."

That was just what Jack would have expected him to say. Unlike the town of Hughes, the college could afford both a good cop and a bad cop.

"I think there is," Jack said. "I think I'm about to get some bad news here, and I don't deserve it."

"It's not bad news," Fieldstone said. "We just want you to take a little vacation. With pay, of course. Why would anyone object to a paid vacation?"

"Have you talked to Dr. Good about that?"

"That's not necessary," Fieldstone said. "Dr. Naylor is her supervisor, and he's already agreed to the decision."

"Nothing like due process," Jack said.

"What was that?"

"Nothing," Jack said.

"You can appeal the decision, Jack," Naylor said. "You certainly have that right. But it could make things very difficult for the college."

"What about me?" Jack asked. "If you take me out of the classroom, people are going to believe you think I'm guilty of something, whether I am or not."

"I'm sure everyone will understand," Naylor said.

"Then you have a lot more faith in people than I do. Besides, *I* don't understand. And I don't like being thrown out of my own classroom. The students won't like it, either. They like consistency when it comes to little things like tests and grading."

"I'm sure you'll be back in the classroom within a couple of days," Naylor said. "After all, the Hughes police force is quite competent. They'll have the real killer in jail before you know it."

"You have a lot more faith in the police around here than I do, too. Remember the last time they had a murder to investigate?"

Neither Naylor nor Fieldstone liked being reminded of the last time. Some of the things that had come out during the investigation of Val Hurley's death hadn't been exactly flattering to the school. And of course the Hughes police hadn't really cracked the case. Sally Good had done that pretty much on her own.

"This won't be like the last time," Fieldstone said. "This time the college won't be involved at all."

Jack couldn't quite believe what he'd heard. He said, "The college is already involved. I'm part of the college, and I've been taken to the police station and questioned. Now you're about to jerk me out of my classroom. How can you say the college isn't involved?"

"*Jerk* isn't exactly the right word," Naylor said. "We're just asking you to take a couple of days off—with pay, remember—and wait for the police to do their job."

"Who's going to take my place in class if I go along with this?"

"That would be me," Naylor said. "I minored in English, as you may know."

Jack knew, all right. He also knew that Naylor hadn't been inside a classroom in fifteen years except maybe to check and see if anyone had stolen a pencil sharpener.

"Besides," Naylor said, "this is Friday. I'm sure the police will have everything wrapped up before we get back here on Monday morning. You probably won't have to miss any classes at all."

Jack wished he shared some of Naylor's touching faith in the abilities of local law enforcement.

"It's not as if you really have any choice in this," Fieldstone said. "The decision has already been made. I don't want any calls from students or their parents after they see the newspaper tomorrow."

"I suppose I could take this up with the faculty senate," Jack said.

"You could do that," Fieldstone agreed. "But I don't think you'll find that it's a good idea."

"You don't think the group will support me?"

"I'm sure you'd have a great deal of support. I just don't think it's in the best interests of the school."

"What about my best interests?"

"We're thinking of you in all this, Jack," Naylor said. "If you went into that classroom, no matter how much your students may like you and trust you, there would be at least a couple of them who'd be suspicious of you and think you didn't belong there."

"Just the ones who are failing," Jack said.

"You know that's not true," Naylor said. "You know how people are."

Jack knew all right. Naylor might as well have been talking about himself and Fieldstone. Jack wanted to protest, but he was getting tired of all the talk about the school's best interests, not to mention his own. Naylor and Fieldstone were going to force him out of his classroom, and that was that. By the time the faculty senate met, which couldn't possibly happen much earlier than Monday afternoon, the damage would already be done.

"All right," he sighed. "I'll do it your way."

"I knew we could count on you," Naylor said.

If that was supposed to make Jack feel better, it didn't work at all.

9

Sally was correcting papers when Jack came into her office, though her mind wasn't really on the job. Fortunately that didn't matter much with multiple-choice tests. She shoved the papers aside, getting them mixed up with another set. Oh, well. She could sort them out later.

"You don't look happy," she said as Jack plopped himself down in the chair beside her desk.

"I'm not." He proceeded to tell her what had happened in Fieldstone's office.

"I'm not surprised," Sally said when he was done.

"Me neither. Just a little disappointed."

"You have to try to see it from their perspective."

Jack stiffened and straightened in the chair. Then he relaxed and smiled.

"For a second there I thought you were serious," he said. "I thought you'd be more upset than this."

"I'm upset. Don't think I'm not. How dare they tell me what to do about one of my own faculty members without consulting me!"

"Have they actually told you yet?"

"No, but I'm sure they'll get around to it. Why don't we go have some lunch so they can't get me on the phone?"

"Good idea," Jack said. "We can eat in the cafeteria. That'll get me in the mood for prison food."

"Now who's not being serious?"

"Gallows humor," Jack said. "I'm getting pretty good at it."

"Not as good as you think," Sally told him.

The cafeteria's Friday specials offered a choice between fish sticks, cole slaw, and french fries, or a chopped barbecue beef sandwich with potato salad on the side.

"Talk about the horns of a dilemma," Jack said as he looked at the menu board.

Sally wasn't impressed by the choices either, but she went for the sandwich. That way she didn't have to deal with nearly as much grease. Or so she thought until she got the sandwich, which was mostly fat and gristle.

Jack got a sandwich, too, and joined Sally at a Formica-topped table. He sat down and looked around the cafeteria. It was very quiet. There were only two other people in sight, both of them part-time instructors. Jack opened up his sandwich and looked inside.

"And they wonder why so few people eat here," he said.

"It could be worse," Sally said.

"It could?"

"We could get ptomaine from the potato salad."

Jack looked at the salad, which was a bright yellow with green chunks that might have been pickles.

"Prison food might not be so bad after all," he said.

"No more prison jokes," Sally ordered. "You're not going to prison, and that's that."

"Dean Naylor feels the same way. He's sure that Weems is going to have this murder solved by Monday. I'll bet he hopes so, but I have my doubts. I'm going to drop a couple of reams of notes for my classes on his desk before I go home this afternoon."

"That'll teach him."

"OK, so it's petty. I admit it. But I'm feeling petty about now."

Sally took a bite of her sandwich. It wasn't quite as bad as it looked. But it wasn't good. She chewed it thoroughly.

"You'll get over it," she said when she could talk again.

"Maybe," Jack mumbled, his mouth half-full of sandwich. "Maybe not. Weems has me down as the killer. He's not going to look very hard for anyone else."

"Then I guess we'll have to," Sally said.

"I don't think Weems would appreciate our help."

"Does that bother you?"

"Not as much as going to prison."

"So what do you say?"

"I guess Weems could use our able assistance. That still doesn't mean he's going to like it."

"I can deal with that."

"Then so can I."

"Fine," Sally said. "Let's get started."

"Aren't you going to finish your sandwich?"

"I don't think so."

"Me neither," Jack said.

The college was very quiet. A former dean had once said that you could shoot a shotgun down the hallway of any building on the Hughes campus on any given Friday afternoon and not hit a soul. Sally could vouch for the truth of that, though she often stayed in her office to get all her papers graded before she left for the weekend. English teachers, even if they were teaching only three classes, which was her load, always had a lot of grading to do. She often wondered how those who taught the regular load of five classes could keep up. And because the school allowed faculty members to teach an extra class, the ones who really needed the money taught six classes. Sally's mind reeled when she thought of all the papers that someone teaching six classes would have to read and mark, but somehow everyone managed to do it, and to do a good job.

"Where do we start?" Jack asked when they were seated in Sally's office.

"What was it Alice said?" Sally asked.

"Alice? Who's Alice?"

"Alice in Wonderland."

"Oh. What's she got to do with this?"

"You asked where we should start, which is what my students always want to know about their essays. I usually give them Alice's advice."

"I'm with you now," Jack said. "It's something about 'you begin at the beginning and keep on going until you come to the end; then you stop.' "

"Close enough," Sally said. "A lot better than my students. Most of them have never heard of Alice in Wonderland."

"I know what you mean. Most of mine haven't even heard about Harry Potter, but that's what makes our jobs so interesting. Anyway, where's the beginning of our problem? Or maybe I should say *my* problem."

Sally thought about that. She said, "Why don't we start with the knife-making class? Whatever possessed you to make a knife? And I want a straight answer this time."

"It all started with a book," Jack said. "I'm an English teacher, after all, and I read a lot, unlike most of our students. In fact, you could say I became an English teacher because I liked to read so much."

"It happens to a lot of us," Sally said, "but we spend so much time grading papers and teaching classes and preparing to teach classes that we hardly ever have time to read."

"Not me. I always make time to read, no matter what."

"Good. I do, too. What was the name of the book?"

"*The Iron Mistress*. It's by Paul Wellman. He also wrote *The Comancheros*."

"Wasn't that a John Wayne movie?"

"Right. A long time ago. You've probably seen it on TV." Jack grew animated. "There's a great scene where Wayne, Stuart Whitman, and Wayne's son, Patrick, are hunkered down behind an over-turned wagon or something, and they're all firing at the bad guys, who come charging at the wagon and jump over it on their horses, and—"

"And Whitman, Wayne, and young Patrick whirl around and drop all three of them," Sally finished.

"That's right! Great scene, just great."

"But it's not from *The Iron Mistress*."

"Nope. That was a movie, too, though, even longer ago than *The Comancheros*. It starred Alan Ladd."

"I vaguely remember him."

"He was short," Jack said. "But then what Hollywood star isn't?"

"John Wayne?"

"Right. Anyway, *The Iron Mistress* is about Jim Bowie."

"Now we're getting somewhere," Sally said. "You read about Jim Bowie, the testosterone started flowing, and you decided you had to make your own Bowie knife."

"Well, that's not exactly right. But I guess it's close enough. The college was offering the course in the continuing ed department, and I thought 'Why not?' How was I to know that the knife would end up in Ralph Bostic's back?"

Sally didn't like to think about that part of it, and she was sure Jack didn't, either. It was hard to believe that a knife Jack had made with his own hands had been used to murder someone, but that was what had happened.

"Tell me about the knife," she said.

"It wasn't easy to make, that's for sure. The class lasted twelve weeks, and we started out by getting our materials. We were given the choice of using old chainsaw blades or leaf springs from junked cars, because springs and chainsaw blades are both made out of good-quality steel. I used a leaf spring. I had to draw the knife on the spring, grind it to shape, temper it—did you know that when you heat metal hot enough, it's not magnetic? That's how you know when you've gotten it hot enough. Anyway—"

"Never mind," Sally said, a little surprised at Jack's enthusiasm.

"I think I have the general idea. Now all we have to do is figure out how the knife got from your office into Bostic's back. Where did you keep the knife?"

"I was sort of proud of it. It looked a lot better than I thought it would. I made the handle out of—"

"Never mind about the handle. You're like a freshman writer who can't stick to the outline."

Jack looked chastened, and Sally was sorry she'd said anything. It was nice to see someone get enthusiastic about something he'd created.

"I didn't mean to criticize," she said.

"Well, you're right. I'm getting way off the subject. I kept the knife right out on the desk where I could see it, and where other people could see it, too. I guess I was hoping someone would ask me about it." Jack smiled sheepishly. "As you can tell, I like talking about it. That's probably why I put my initials on the blade, too. I wish I hadn't done that."

"When did the knife disappear?" Sally asked.

"It was about three weeks ago," Jack said. "I came back from class one day, and it wasn't there. Anyone could have stopped by my office and slipped it under a shirt or in a purse and been out of there. It wouldn't have taken more than a few seconds."

"You said you put it on the desk so other people would ask you about it. Didn't you think that might be dangerous? What if an irate student had grabbed it and sliced you up with it?"

"I don't usually have any irate students," Jack said.

That was true, Sally reflected. She might have complaints about some of her other faculty members, but no one ever had a problem with Jack. His student evaluations were always highly favorable, and students flocked to his classes. That wasn't true of other faculty members she could name, some of whom were jealous of the fact that Jack never had to worry about filling his classes.

"You're lucky," she said. "But it was still dangerous. Did anyone ever mention the knife?"

"There weren't many who did," Jack said. "I was a little disappointed."

Sally smiled. "As I'd say to my freshmen, be more specific."

"Right. Let's see. You never asked about it, that's for sure."

"I'm not very interested in knives."

"I don't blame you. I wish I hadn't been. Jorge Rodriguez was, though. He stopped by one day, and we must've talked for half an hour. He knew a little about knife-making."

Sally couldn't help but be curious. "He did?"

"It's something that interests a lot of inmates," Jack said. "They make them out of just about everything: spoons, pieces of wire, plastic combs, you name it."

"Oh," Sally said.

"Jorge and Bostic didn't like each other much, did they," Jack said.

"No," Sally said. "They didn't get along at all."

10

"Of course nobody really liked Bostic," Jack said. "So there's no need to start thinking that Jorge might've killed him."

Sally knew that, but she couldn't help it. There was a definite flaw in her character when it came to Jorge. On the one hand, she was attracted to him; on the other hand, she was sure she shouldn't be, and she was automatically suspicious of him when bad things happened.

"There's Roy Don Talon, for one," Sally said, trying to get her mind off Jorge. She went on to tell Jack what she'd learned from Wynona. "I wonder who we could ask about that."

"How about Talon?"

Sally wasn't sure she wanted to be so direct. Talon was on the college board of trustees, after all, and Fieldstone frowned on faculty members talking about school matters with members of the board. She said as much to Jack.

"You're right about that," he agreed. "Fieldstone made it pretty clear to me in his office that he didn't want the college to be involved in this in any way. If we talk to Talon, he'll probably just throw us out of his office, and then he'll be on the phone to Fieldstone tattling on us before the door swings shut."

Sally thought about that, and something else occurred to her, something she should have thought of before.

"That contract Bostic had to repair the college vehicles," she said. "Surely the board should have known about it. Those things aren't secrets. A. B. D. shouldn't have had to tell them about it."

"You're right again," Jack said. "Of course, stuff like that can be buried in documents and double-talk if you handle it right. So it's barely possible that none of the board knew."

Sally didn't really believe that. Someone knew. Someone had worked it out and gotten it approved. The business manager surely must have known. He had to approve all the contracts. Sally didn't like the direction her thoughts were taking her, but she had to voice them.

"Fieldstone knew," she said. "He knows everything. And Hal Kaul knew."

Kaul was the business manager. He was a short man with thinning, straw-colored hair, and he always had a pencil stuck behind one ear. No one had ever seen him use the pencil. He did all his writing with a ballpoint pen that he kept in his shirt pocket. Nevertheless, the pencil was always there.

"There might be ways to get things done without Kaul or Fieldstone knowing," Jack said.

"There might be, but someone had to get it done."

"That's an angle to look at, then. It's all pretty ironic, isn't it?"

"In what way?"

"Bostic won his board seat by telling everybody that he stood for fiscal responsibility. He said he was going to see to it that the college was run like a business. And now we know he was guilty of profiteering at the college's expense."

"And you're surprised?"

"Not really. Besides, he made good on his promise, at least partially. He was running the vehicle repairs like a business. His business, that is."

"Do you think that's why he was killed?" Sally asked.

"It could be, but you're forgetting something. Fieldstone might be right."

"About what?"

"This murder might not have anything to do with the college.

Bostic must have had enemies all over town, given the kind of person he was. What if one of them killed him?"

"I suppose we'll have to find out about his personal life, too," Sally said.

She was getting discouraged already. She wasn't a trained investigator. She didn't know anything about police techniques. Why couldn't Weems just do his job?

Maybe he would, she thought. Maybe she and Jack were overreacting. That was easy for her to think, though. She wasn't the one who'd been accused of murder.

But why did she feel so loyal to Jack? How did she know that he hadn't done the killing himself? Maybe she was guilty of letting her emotions get in the way of her logic. After all, Jack had asked her out, and she had accepted his invitation. She hadn't dated many men since the death of her husband six years earlier, so there was clearly something about Jack that she found attractive. Not in the same way that she found Jorge attractive, she had to admit, but then Jorge hadn't asked her out.

Sally shook her head. She was letting her mind wander, getting off the topic, the same thing she had accused Jack of doing.

"Do we know anyone who could tell us about Bostic?" she asked.

Jack's eyes moved in the same direction that Sally's did, toward Naylor's outer office.

"Wynona," they both said together.

Wynona didn't see them coming because she was concentrating on a crossword puzzle. She put it down hurriedly when Jack tapped on the door frame.

"I was just taking a little break," she said. "I get a ten-minute break every afternoon. It's part of the job description. You can look it up."

"Don't mind us," Sally said. "Enjoy your break. Is the dean in?"

"No," Wynona said. "He's out."

Sally knew very well that Naylor was out. Otherwise, Wynona

wouldn't have been working on the puzzle, break or no break, even though it was Friday afternoon and no one else was around. Sally, however, knew better than to say anything like that to Wynona.

"I'm sorry we missed him," Sally said. "We wanted to talk to him about Ralph Bostic."

Wynona was instantly alert.

"What about Ralph Bostic?" she asked.

"Oh, nothing much. It wasn't about college business. I was just wondering about Bostic's personal life. You know, because of the murder. But I don't suppose you'd know anything about that."

She was pretty sure that Wynona did know about Bostic's personal life. He was a member of the board, and Wynona would have made it her business to find out about him. Because Sally didn't have anything to trade this time, she was hoping to appeal to Wynona's vanity.

It worked.

"You'd probably be surprised at some of the things I know," Wynona said.

"I'm sure I would," Sally said. "This doesn't really concern the college, though."

"I've lived in Hughes for more than fort—well, a long time," Wynona said, catching herself just before she revealed her age. "It's a small town, and you know how people in a small town can talk. They don't spend much of their time talking about the college, believe me. There are a lot of other things going on around here."

"Such as?"

"Such as Ralph Bostic's love life, for one thing."

"That sounds interesting," Sally said, giving Jack a glance to see if he was taking it all in. He gave her a slight nod to let her know he wasn't missing anything. "What about it?"

"I'm sure you know he was having an affair with one of our faculty members."

Sally tried not to look surprised, but the truth was that she hadn't known any such thing. She didn't think Troy Beauchamp knew it, either, or he would have told her. Not knowing might not bother him, though, since the affair was certain to have been conducted discreetly off campus. Still, it was something Troy would usually have known about.

Jack wasn't quite as cool as Sally. He said, "Who on earth?"

Wynona waggled a finger at him and smiled redly. Sally wondered where the secretary found lipstick of that peculiarly bright shade.

"That would be telling too much," Wynona said. "I have to keep some things secret."

"No you don't," Jack said.

"You're keeping secrets from me," Wynona told him. "You haven't mentioned a thing about your trip to the jail this morning."

Sally nudged Jack with her elbow, and he said, "What would you like to know?"

"All about it," Wynona said.

Jack gave her the short version and finished by saying, "I have to prove I'm not guilty, and that's why we have to find out about Bostic. Right now I'm the only suspect."

"I know," Wynona said. "Dr. Good told me."

"Then you know why I need all the information I can get," Jack said. "Now tell us who Bostic's having an affair with "

Wynona thought about it for a while, and Sally wondered if she should correct Jack's grammar. Probably not. He was upset enough already, and he probably would have phrased things differently, given the time to think about it.

Wynona finally said, "Mae Wilkins."

"Oh my God," Sally said before she could catch herself.

Mae was one of the instructors in the English department. She was the Hughes College version of Martha Stewart, always immaculate, every hair in place. Her office was a miracle of order, with all her syllabi neatly squared away in wall shelves, the books arranged in alphabetical order by author or editor, and there were fresh flowers on Mae's desk every day. She sold Mary Kay cosmetics on the side and apparently did very well at it, as she drove a pink Cadillac.

Wynona leaned back, grinning in satisfaction at the surprise on Sally and Jack's faces.

"I know it's hard to believe," Wynona said. "Ralph Bostic always looked like he'd been changing spark plugs with his bare hands, and his pants looked like he'd been using them to clean dipsticks. It's hard to imagine what Mae saw in him."

Sally still couldn't quite believe it.

"Are you sure it's true?" she said.

Wynona looked hurt. She stuck out her lower lip and pretended to pout, a look that didn't really suit her.

"I'm sorry," Sally said. "I know you wouldn't tell me anything that wasn't true. But May and Ralph Bostic? Opposites attract, I suppose."

"You got me," Wynona said. "I like cowboys, myself."

Sally didn't want to get into what Wynona liked. She was afraid she might find out more than she wanted to know on that topic.

"Is there anything else you can tell us?"

"Well," Wynona said, "there's the rumor about the hot-car ring."

This time it was Jack who couldn't help exclaiming.

"Good grief! Was he stealing cars?"

"I wouldn't know about that part of it," Wynona said. "All I know is that some people think he was mixed up in getting stolen cars across the border to Mexico, where they were sold. I'd have thought you might know about that one, since some people on campus did."

"Who?" Sally asked.

"President Fieldstone. He was going to use the information to get Bostic off the board."

Sally didn't have to ask the source of that story. It had to be Naylor.

"And of course Bostic was trying to keep the board from renewing Fieldstone's contract."

Sally and Jack had run out of things to say. They just looked at one another.

"That's about all, I guess," Wynona said. "I told you I knew things."

"You weren't kidding," Sally said.

11

———

She certainly gave us plenty to think about," Jack said as they walked back to Sally's office.

"Yes," Sally said. "Too much. We're out of our depth here, Jack. We need to call Weems."

Jack followed Sally through the office door and plopped back down in the chair by her desk.

"I really wish you hadn't said that," he told her.

"You know I'm right about it. I can deal with hot love affairs. But hot-car rings? No thanks."

"I didn't think a pistol-packing woman like you would let a little thing like a hot-car ring bother you."

"You know about the pistol?"

"Everybody knows about the pistol," Jack said.

Sally was a little surprised, though she knew she shouldn't have been. It was beginning to appear that there was no such thing as a secret in Hughes, Texas.

Not that she minded people knowing about the pistol. She wasn't ashamed of it. It was a Smith & Wesson Model 36, the Ladysmith with a three-inch barrel and wood-grain grips. She kept it in a burgundy carrying case, which she felt was appropriate for a lady.

Sally had taken a concealed handgun course offered by the college, not because she'd read a book but because she was curious.

And to her mild astonishment she had found out that she liked guns. She knew that wasn't a politically correct thing to do, and it wasn't as if she had become a militant supporter of the NRA. She wasn't in the least afraid that the government was going to send a squad of jackbooted thugs to break into her house, shoot her full of holes with their automatic rifles, and pry her Ladysmith from her cold dead fingers. She simply liked guns, particularly pistols. She liked the way they were made, the way they fit her hand, the way she could take out her frustrations after a hard day by blasting away at the silhouettes on the targets at the school's range.

Besides, she had discovered that she had a natural talent for shooting. She started out well, and she got even better. Even at that, however, she never felt an urge to go hunting or to use the pistol for anything other than target practice. If she had to, she supposed she might use it for self-defense, but the occasion to do that had never arisen. She thought that was just as well. She'd heard that some people were unable to pull the trigger when it came to shooting another human being, and she might well be one of them.

Anyway, it wasn't as if she carried the pistol with her. She kept it in the lingerie drawer of her dresser, and when she took it to the shooting range, she put it in the trunk of her car. If that was "packing," then she was guilty.

"What do you want me to do?" she asked Jack. "Shoot somebody? Somebody specific?"

Jack smiled. He had a nice smile, Sally thought. Sort of like one of those self-effacing movie stars from the old days, the kind of guy who probably couldn't get a part in a movie now that brashness was all.

"I don't want you to shoot anybody," he said. "I just thought you could protect me from the hot-car ring if I had to confront any of the members."

"I don't think I'd be very good at that. That's a job for the police."

"I know. I guess I was just hoping that we could find some way to get me out of this mess."

"What about an alibi?" Sally asked. "Did Weems ask you for one?"

"Of course," Jack said. "But it wasn't much help. When Bostic was killed, I was at home, reading. Alone."

Sally didn't read a lot of mystery novels, but she'd read enough to know that being at home alone wasn't much of an alibi. In fact, it wasn't any kind of an alibi at all.

"What about phone calls?" she asked. "Did you phone anyone? Did anyone phone you?"

"I don't get a lot of calls," Jack said. "I don't make many, either." He paused. "Wait a minute! I did get a call last night, from my mother. She always wants to know if I'm getting enough to eat."

"My mother's the same way," Sally said, thinking that mothers were like that, even if their children were long grown and even a few pounds overweight. "What time did she call?"

"Too early," Jack said, shaking his head. "Bostic was killed between nine and ten, or at least that's the impression I got. I got the call around eight-thirty."

"So much for that alibi," Sally said.

"I could be wrong about the time of the call. I didn't look at the clock. I could give my mother a ring and ask her about it."

"Won't she ask why?"

"Naturally. That's okay, though. I just need to let her know about my problems before she sees them on TV or reads about them in the papers."

"There shouldn't be much in the papers yet. Weems probably won't give out your name."

"But he might. You never know what a guy like that will do. Besides, there's probably some record of my little visit to the police station, official or not. Some reporter will sniff it out if it's there, and my mother reads the papers from front to back every day. If my name's in there, she'll find it."

"Will she be worried about you?"

"Isn't that what mothers do? Worry?"

"Most of them, probably. And with good reason in this case. So do you want to call Weems and tell him what we've found out, or should I?"

"Why don't you do it," Jack said. "He won't listen to me. He'll think I'm just trying to create confusion and cover up for myself. Which I guess is the truth, more or less."

Sally picked up the phone and dialed. She got Weems fairly quickly after talking to only a couple of people at the police station, but she could tell he wasn't happy to hear from her. He was even less happy when she told him what she wanted.

"Dr. Good," he said, "you're an intelligent person, what with your degrees and everything. You should know better than to interfere with a police investigation."

"I'm not interfering," Sally said. "I'm just offering you some information that might help you."

"Let's say I came in your classroom one day and started telling you how to teach *Beowulf* because I've read this new translation and might have some information that would help you. Would you call that interfering?"

Sally didn't like the idea of anyone coming into her classroom to tell her how to teach, but she didn't want to say so. She thought about Naylor taking over Jack's classes and wondered if the dean would consider that interfering. Probably not, but Jack would, and with plenty of justification, to Sally's way of thinking.

"Dr. Good?" Weems said. "You still there?"

"All right, you have a point," Sally said.

"You're damned right I do. And that's how I feel when some public-spirited citizen such as yourself tries to tell me how to run an investigation. You and your boyfriend need to back off and let me do my job."

Boyfriend? Sally thought, looking at Jack, who was staring at her bookshelves. *Boyfriend?*

"Dr. Good? Are you drifting off again?"

"No," Sally said. "I'm right here. I won't be bothering you anymore."

"That's the best news I've had all day," Weems said.

70

Sally hung up the telephone and looked at Jack, who was smiling wryly.

"I told you so," Jack said.

"You don't have to remind me. What do you think about Bostic trying to have Fieldstone fired?"

"According to Wynona, Bostic was just trying to talk the board into not renewing the contract. That's not the same thing as having someone fired. I'm sure Fieldstone's contract has several years yet to run. He could find another job long before it expired, if he wanted to."

"What if he didn't want to? What if he wanted to hang on here at Hughes until he was ready to retire?"

"I don't know," Jack said.

"Did Fieldstone ever stop by your office to admire your home-made knife?"

"As a matter of fact, he did come by one day. He was on his way to a meeting."

Fieldstone didn't make it a habit to spend much time with the faculty. He always said that he believed in leaving them alone to do their jobs, though he would occasionally visit their offices when he was passing through the building.

"Did he mention the knife?"

"Yes," Jack said. "Or maybe I mentioned it. Somebody did. I told him about making it."

"What about Mae Wilkins?"

"You're kidding. You think she'd admire a knife?"

"I just wondered if she'd seen it."

"As a matter of fact, she told me once how tacky she thought it was. You don't think she killed Bostic with it, do you? I think that if she ever killed anyone, she'd use poison, not some tacky handmade knife. Besides, guns and knives are way too messy for her."

"You're right, I guess. I was just thinking, though, that everyone who's mixed up with Bostic has seen that knife in your office."

"You didn't mention Hal Kaul. He saw it, too."

"He was in this building?" Sally asked. Kaul left his office even less often than Fieldstone did.

"Meeting," Jack said.

"Oh. Well, that just makes it tougher."

"Makes what tougher?"

"Finding out who killed Bostic."

"You mean we're not turning it over to the cops?"

"We tried," Sally said. "Weems wouldn't listen. Remember?"

"I told you so."

"Don't start that again. No one likes a smart-aleck."

"I'm not so smart. If I were smart, I wouldn't be taking a paid vacation from my classes, starting next week."

"Nobody who leaves a knife lying around on his desk is a genius, but you haven't started that paid vacation yet."

"I've learned an important lesson about knives," Jack said.

"I certainly hope so," Sally told him.

"Trust me. Now what about the paid vacation?"

"If you're not going to take it, we'd better get busy."

"So what do we do first?"

"That's a good question," Sally said, "and I don't have an answer for it."

"Neither do I."

"Just in case, you'd probably better go make out those tons of lesson plans for Naylor."

"I was afraid you'd say that," Jack told her.

12

It took Jack nearly an hour, but he built up quite an impressive stack of material for Naylor's use in the classroom. Jack was going to insist that Naylor had to cover every single syllable of it. While he worked he looked at the place on his desk where the knife had sat, thinking about what a dunce he'd been to leave it there. It had been a really nice knife, though. He'd been proud of the workmanship and not a little surprised that he'd been able to turn out something so well made.

The more he thought about the knife, however, the more something bothered him. Unfortunately, he couldn't figure out just what was causing the bother, other than that it was something about the knife. Maybe he was just confused. It had, after all, been a confusing day. He'd never been accused of murder and grilled by the cops before.

He gathered up all his materials, stuffing papers into separate folders for each class, but Naylor still wasn't back in his office when Jack arrived with his mound of paperwork. Wynona said that she expected the dean back at any minute, but Jack didn't want to wait around. He wrote Naylor a short note and left everything with Wynona.

"I'll see that he gets it," she said.

"Thanks," Jack said, and headed back to Sally's office.

She was still there, grading tests. When Jack came to the door, she looked up and said, "Everything taken care of?"

"I think so. Naylor should have a very busy weekend, if he even bothers to look at the stuff I gave him."

"I'm sure he will. He's very conscientious."

"Great," Jack said. "Maybe my students won't even care if I'm indicted for murder. They can keep Naylor for the rest of the semester."

"Don't talk like that. I called Mae Wilkins but she's not in her office."

"It's Friday afternoon," Jack pointed out. He looked at his watch. "In fact, it's after four o'clock on Friday afternoon. There's no one here except us, the secretaries, and the deans. And I'm not so sure about one of the deans."

"Then we should leave," Sally said.

"Good idea. Then what?"

"We'll have to think about that. What would be a good place to do some thinking?"

"The Seahorse Club?" Jack said.

There were no bars in Hughes, but there were "private clubs" that anyone with a couple of bucks could join. Under the law, members of the private clubs could be served alcohol. The Seahorse had the advantage of being near the college campus. That was also its disadvantage. It was the preferred place for college faculty to have a drink, and Jack wasn't sure Sally would want to be seen with him. For that matter, he wasn't sure he wanted to be seen by anyone. He'd have to answer too many questions, and there wouldn't be any time to consider what he and Sally should do, if anything, about his problems. He was surprised that Troy Beauchamp hadn't already sought him out to pump him for information.

"The Seahorse is a little too public," Sally said, echoing Jack's thoughts. "Why don't we go to my house?"

That sounded fine to Jack. He was pretty sure that any chance of romantic involvement was dead now that he was a murder suspect, but he'd take whatever he could get.

"I'll get my car and follow you," he said. "I'm not parked far from you."

As they were walking out to the parking lot, they passed under the big oak tree near the shop building where both auto mechanics and welding classes were taught. The auto mechanics and welding shop was on the opposite side of the campus from the administration building, and the parking lot beside it was a bit more convenient for Jack and Sally. When the welders were working, taking a peek into one of the building's small windows was a little like glancing into the infernal regions, where masked demons moved around among the sparks and blue flames.

"That's where I did a lot of work on the knife," Jack said, flipping a hand in the direction of the building. "I heated the blade to temper it with an acetylene torch."

"Who taught that knife-making class?" Sally asked.

"Stanley Owens. You probably don't know him. He teaches just that one class in continuing ed. I don't think he has a degree. Nice looking, with really gray hair. His real job is office management. He manages the repair department for your friend Roy Don Talon."

"He's not exactly my friend."

"Irony," Jack said. "That's what we English teachers call it."

"Oh," Sally said.

"Talon is on campus occasionally. Sometimes he stops by to say hello. I think he came to a faculty workshop one fall. Sat in the back row of the meeting room and never said a word, which is pretty odd when you consider his occupation."

"I get it," Sally said. "Irony. Because he's a car salesman, and they tend to be talkative."

"Right the first time. Maybe you should consider becoming an English teacher. Anyway, I'm sure Fieldstone wishes that all the members of the faculty kept their mouths shut."

"Unlike those of you who are accused killers and speak up at board meetings."

"That's one way to put it," Jack said.

Sally looked at the automotive building. She'd been on the Hughes campus for six years now, but she'd never even looked inside the shop. She wondered what went on in there.

"I've never been inside that building," she said. "Let's have a look."

"It's Friday afternoon," Jack reminded her. "There won't be anyone around."

"I'm not interested in interviewing the faculty. I just thought it might be interesting to see what it looks like."

Jack shrugged and said, "I don't see any reason why we can't have a look."

They went over to the heavy steel door, and Jack pulled it open, holding it for Sally to walk through. He was never sure whether a man should do things like that for a woman these days, and he hoped she wouldn't think less of him.

The inside of the building smelled of oil and gas and something that might have been antifreeze or possibly power-steering fluid. Sally wasn't an expert in automotive smells.

No lights were on, and because the building's designers had hoped to cut down on cooling costs by reducing the number and size of the windows, it was hard to see anything. Sally didn't know where the light switch was, though she thought it should be somewhere near the door. Jack was fumbling around for it when she heard something scrape softly on the concrete floor.

Jack stopped groping for the light switch.

"Did you hear that?" he whispered.

"Why are you whispering?" Sally asked.

Jack spoke up a bit. "I don't know. It just seemed like the thing to do."

"Is anyone there?" Sally called.

There was no answer. She looked around the large, gloomy area. She could see a little better now that her eyes were getting adjusted. There was some illumination from the small windows, and the edges of the large doors on the opposite side of the shop were lined with daylight.

There was only one car in the shop, a fairly new model that Sally couldn't identify. It sat off to one side where it appeared to have been freshly painted. There was a sharp smell of paint in the stuffy room.

Nearby there was some kind of portable hoist, with an engine hanging dangling from it by chains. There was a hydraulic lift that was raised for no reason that Sally could see. It was as if someone were changing the oil on an invisible car. There was also a square hole in the floor with steel tracks across it. Sally thought it might be a grease pit, though why it was necessary when there was a lift, she didn't know. On the wall beside the car there were some large metal toolboxes on wheels and a couple of immobile steel lockers.

On the opposite side of the shop stood the acetylene bottles and some of the welding equipment, with which Sally was completely unfamiliar, not that she could have identified it anyway in the dim light. There were a couple of workbenches with tools on them and vises affixed to each end. A few wrenches and a couple of hubcaps lay on the floor beneath them.

"Maybe we were just imagining things," she said.

"Both of us at the same time?" Jack said.

"Well, I don't see anyone. Do you?"

Jack said that he didn't, and Sally called out again. There was still no response.

"What about the lights?" she said.

Jack again felt around on the wall for the switch.

"Here it is," he said, and Sally heard a muted click.

The lights didn't come on. There were another couple of clicks, but the result was the same: no lights.

"I think it's time to go," Jack said. "There's nothing to see in here, anyway."

There was another low sound, as if something had brushed softly against a wall.

"Someone's in here," Sally said. "Hey! Who's there?"

No one replied.

"Probably a cat," Jack said. "Maybe even a rat. You never know. Let's get out of here."

"Just a minute," Sally said. "I'm sure there's someone in here."

There weren't too many places to hide other than the car and the area around the workbenches and the acetylene bottles. Sally started toward the benches. Jack trailed along behind her.

When they passed the square pit in the floor, Sally looked down. The bottom of the hole was five or six feet below floor level. There were a few rags lying down there, along with what looked like a small metal toolbox.

And there was one other thing.

"Is there someone down there?" she said.

Jack stopped beside her and looked.

"Damn," he said.

Both of them moved a little closer to the edge of the hole.

"Hey," Jack said, but the figure lying below them didn't move.

"We'd better go for help," Jack said.

"But there's someone in here," Sally said.

"Yeah. He's lying down there in the grease pit, and he's not moving."

"*Some*body's moving," Sally said.

"All the more reason that we should go for help, if you ask me."

Sally knew he was right, and she knew all those sayings about curiosity and cats. None of that seemed to matter right at the moment, however. She really wanted to know who was in there with them.

"Come on," she said.

They had gotten to within about ten feet of the acetylene bottles when one of the bottles fell over with a terrible ringing sound, and they were suddenly confronted by the creature from the black lagoon.

13

The creature roared and shambled toward them, waving a ball-peen hammer menacingly.

Sally realized at that moment that she wasn't seeing some movie monster at all but a human being. Monsters didn't carry hammers—not ballpeen hammers, anyway. Maybe claw hammers, but definitely not the ballpeen variety.

But people did, even when they were wearing a welder's helmet, jacket, and gloves.

That was all Sally had time to think before the helmeted figure shoved her to the floor, causing her to scrape her hands and knees on the oil-stained concrete. Jack tried to stop the charging figure, but he was flattened by a solid side-body block. He got up quickly, however, and made a running jump, landing squarely on the figure's back, wrapping his arm around the helmet.

The temporarily blinded figure stumbled forward, trying to fling Jack away and at the same time swinging an arm behind its back in an attempt to hit Jack with the hammer. To Sally's amazement, Jack managed to hang on until both he and the figure yelled and disappeared from Sally's view as they fell forward into the grease pit.

Jack was momentarily stunned. He knew he was lying on someone, and then he remembered the man in the welder's mask. He tried to regain his grip but stopped when he discovered that he was staring down into the wide-open eyes of Ray Thomas, the college's automotive instructor.

Thomas, in spite of the open eyes, merely appeared to be staring back. He wasn't seeing a thing, and he wouldn't be, ever again.

Almost at the same time Jack realized that Thomas was dead, Jack felt something wet and slick under his hand. He didn't even have to look to know it was blood, or something worse.

Jack recoiled from the clammy body beneath him, jerking himself into a clumsy crouch. He was wiping his hand on his pants when he saw the phantom welder climbing out of the pit on a set of concrete steps. Jack went after him just as Sally appeared and slammed something into the side of the welding helmet.

The man fell backward onto Jack, and they both hit the floor again. This time the back of Jack's head bounced lightly off the concrete, and bright white lights flashed in front of his eyes. His situation wasn't improved any when the welder got up and kicked him in the ribs. Jack groaned and tried to roll away, but the welder got in two more solid kicks before Jack could escape.

Jack got to his knees and tried to hold up his head. The welder moved fast and well for a man his size. He was big, as large as Jorge Rodriguez. But it couldn't be Jorge, Jack told himself. Jorge had already been in prison once. He wouldn't want to go back.

Jack's assailant, whoever it was, was no longer interested in Jack. He was climbing out of the pit again, and this time he was ready for Sally. As his head passed the level of the floor, he put up his arm to block the blow she aimed at him and made a swing at her with the hammer. He missed, as she easily ducked aside and darted backward. The welder emerged from the pit and started toward her.

Jack stood up. It hurt to breathe, and he figured he had a couple of broken ribs. Maybe more than a couple, but that didn't matter. He had to help Sally. He staggered toward the steps and climbed them slowly. A sharp pain stabbed him with every step and every breath.

Jack decided that the sharp edges of his broken ribs were poking into his lungs, which would probably pop like a balloon, causing him to sail around the room like a rapidly deflating cartoon character. A ridiculous image. Maybe his brain was damaged, too.

When he got to the top of the steps he saw that Sally was standing in front of the door, blocking the welder's exit. She was holding something in her hand and waving it in front of her. Every time the welder advanced on her, she swung at him and backed him away from the door.

Jack tried to sneak up on the man from behind, but it was hard for him to move quietly. His breath rasped out throatily, and his feet were scraping on the concrete. He tried to lift his feet higher, but he couldn't.

When he was a couple of feet behind the welder, Sally got lucky and hit the hand with the hammer in it. The hammer spun away, and the welder turned to see where it was going.

He also saw Jack, who had to duck out of the hammer's path. Sally tried to hit the welder in the back of the head, but he tucked his shoulder and plowed into Jack as if he were a Dallas Cowboy lineman clearing a path for Emmitt Smith.

Jack felt all the rest of his ribs crack in half and sat down hard on the floor. A shock traveled all the way up his spine and came out at his eyes. The welder retrieved his hammer as Sally knelt by Jack.

"Are you all right?" she asked.

Jack couldn't help laughing at the question, but the laughter hurt so much that he stopped immediately.

"No," he managed to say.

He tried to stand up, and with Sally's help he made it, though he was so bent at the waist that he looked a little like a crone searching for a broom to ride.

There was a ringing noise, followed by a loud and continuous scuffing. Jack forced his head up for a look.

The maniac welder had dropped his hammer and was pushing the portable chain hoist across the floor. It moved slowly at first, but it picked up speed quickly. The dangling engine was swinging a bit, back and forth, gaining momentum from the movement of the hoist, and it was headed straight for Jack and Sally. Jack could almost feel it crashing into his ribs, what there was left of them.

"Run for it," Jack said, giving Sally a gentle shove only because he couldn't push her aside with any more force.

Sally moved away, trying to pull Jack along with her. Jack went, but it was an excruciating experience. The chain hoist followed right along.

Jack saw that Sally had a lug wrench in her right hand. Jack stopped moving and put a hand on the wrench.

"Let me have that," he said.

Sally let it go, and Jack heaved it at the deranged welder. It flipped over in the air and struck the man right in the faceplate. If Jack had been able to throw it harder, it might actually have done some good. As it was, the wrench bounced harmlessly off the faceplate and clattered on the floor. The chain hoist paused, then started moving again.

"I really don't think that guy likes us," Jack said. "Do you have your cell phone?"

Sally nodded.

"Get down in that grease pit and use it, then."

"Won't work in here," Sally said. "Too much metal in the building."

"Try it," Jack said.

Sally ran for the pit, and Jack tried to lead the hoist away from her. He was as slow as a three-legged turtle, and he was afraid the engine was going to smash into him and finish him off. He'd probably wind up looking like one of those cartoon characters that had been run over by a bulldozer.

As he hobbled, he kicked a hubcap. He stopped to pick it up, then sailed it toward the welder. It flew through the air, looking a bit like a flying saucer in a grade-Z movie. Jack envisioned it chopping the welder's head off at the neck, causing the mask to go bouncing along on the floor.

Things didn't work out quite the way Jack had imagined them, however, because the hubcap never got near the welder. It chinged off one pole of the chain hoist and rattled across the floor, finally righting itself somehow and rolling smoothly for several feet before dropping over the edge of the grease pit. It must have landed on Thomas's body, or maybe on Sally, because it didn't make another sound.

The chain hoist kept right on moving, and Jack braced himself for the impact.

It didn't happen.

The hoist stopped moving while it was still several feet away from Jack, and the welder left it to run for the door. Jack realized that the man hadn't intended to hurt him anymore. All he'd really wanted was a way out.

Jack limped after him, but he couldn't have caught a sluggish snail. The man was outside in moments, and the door swung shut behind him. Jack was still trying to get the door open when Sally came out of the pit to help him.

Together they pulled the door back and looked outside, blinking in the late afternoon light. There was no one in sight. After all, it was Friday afternoon, and the campus was virtually deserted. The welder's mask was lying at their feet where whoever had been wearing it had hastily dropped it. The gloves and jacket were a little farther away, but not much.

Jack leaned back against the rough brick side of the building and slid slowly down it.

Sally sat down beside him. For a while neither of them said anything.

Finally Jack turned to Sally. He tried to smile, which was about the only thing he could do that didn't hurt him, and even that didn't feel so good.

"Who was that masked man?" he said.

14

Jack, who had been taped up tighter than King Tut by the skilled practitioners at the Hughes Hospital emergency room, was sitting in Eric Desmond's office with a can of Pepsi One in one hand and a package of peanut-butter-and-cheese crackers in the other. Jack had often wondered what there was in those crackers to make them such a funny color of orange. Probably better not to think about it.

Jack looked around the office. There were photos of Desmond on all the walls: Desmond riding horses, Desmond crossing the finish line at a 10K race, Desmond receiving some award, Desmond on the firing range wearing ear protection and holding a very large pistol, Desmond (probably a much younger version, though he still looked much the same) leaning out of a military helicopter and waving to someone, maybe the photographer.

"You're supposed to like yourself," Sally said, walking into the office. "It's a sign of a healthy self-concept."

Jack told her that he hadn't heard anyone use the phrase *self-concept* in years. "Are you sure there's not some new phrase for that?"

"I don't keep up," Sally said. "It doesn't seem worth it, somehow." Then she changed the subject. "Weems is pretty upset with us, you know."

"No shit, Sherlock," Jack said. And immediately felt like an idiot. "Sorry. I didn't mean to be crude. That just slipped out. I've been feeling a little weird ever since I hit my head on the floor in the automotive building."

"It's nothing I haven't heard before," Sally said. "And the thought of having to talk to Weems would make anybody want to say a few bad words."

Jack had avoided seeing Weems sooner by virtue of the fact that Sally had called the EMS on her cell phone while Jack sat by the wall and suffered in silence. As she had predicted, the phone hadn't worked inside the shop, but it worked just fine once they got out. She called the EMS first, then Desmond, and then Weems. The EMS had beat Weems to the scene by at least a minute and a half, for which Jack would be eternally grateful.

At the ER, he'd been poked and probed and X rayed and wrapped. To his surprise, he had only two cracked ribs—not broken but cracked—and while they hurt quite a bit, it could have been worse. The tape would hold him together for a while, and then he'd be fine. Or so he'd been told. Jack wasn't sure he trusted a doctor who looked so young that she could have passed for a student at HCC. Besides the cracked ribs, Jack also had a hard little knot on the back of his head, but there was no concussion.

He sipped at his Pepsi, then said, "Weems can't possibly believe I had anything to do with this murder," he said. "Can he?"

"I don't see why not," Sally said. "You're the one with blood on his hands. You're the one whose handprint is going to be right there on the floor by Thomas's body in Thomas's own blood."

"I think it was something besides just blood," Jack said, but he didn't say what it was.

He looked at his hand, palm up. It was clean now, but he easily could imagine that the blood was still there. He could practically see it trapped in the lines that crisscrossed his skin. He knew how Lady Macbeth must've felt.

"I shouldn't have told you about that," he said. "That Weems couldn't possibly think I had anything to do with the murder, I mean."

"Why not?"

"It sounds almost like I was trying to create an alibi. When I think about it, I can see how Weems might figure it: I was supposedly in my office working on the lesson plans for Naylor, but in reality I was out in the automotive building killing Thomas."

"Why would you do that?"

"I don't have a clue, but I'm sure Weems will come up with a reason. That's the way his mind works."

"You don't have any history with Thomas, do you?"

Jack sighed and offered Sally a cheese cracker. She declined, so he ate it himself. The peanut butter gummed up his mouth, and for a few seconds he couldn't talk at all. He took a drink from the Pepsi can, swallowed, and said, "I might."

"You might? What do you mean by 'might'?"

"I guess I mean that I sort of do."

It was Sally's turn to sigh. "For such a mild-mannered man, you seem to make a lot of enemies."

Jack wondered whether it was a compliment to be considered mild-mannered. He decided that he wouldn't ask. He wasn't sure he wanted to know.

"We weren't enemies," he said. "I just had a little disagreement with him. It wasn't even that, exactly."

"What was it, then?"

"Okay, call it a disagreement. It was when I was taking that knife-making class."

"You really should've found a better way to spend your time," Sally said.

"I couldn't agree more. Next time I think I'll take something safer, like recreational bungee jumping."

"What did you disagree with Thomas about?"

"He disagreed with me. He thought I was a bit careless with the torch when I was heating my knife blade. He said I was a menace, or words to that effect."

"Were you?"

"I don't think so, but then I'm not a professional welder. It was the way he said it that upset me."

"Just how upset were you?"

"Well, I might have told him to back off before I set his shirt on fire."

"There's that 'might' again," Sally said.

"Right. Well, that's what I said, more or less. I don't remember the exact words, but that's close enough."

"Did anybody hear you say them?"

"Sure. Several of the class members were there, not to mention the instructor." Jack had another drink of Pepsi. "But why should any of that matter? You saw what happened in there. You even know how the handprint got there, if there is one. Weems would have to be crazy to suspect me."

"You could have set up the whole thing," Sally said. "Just so you could claim me as a witness."

"Who's my accomplice in the welding mask?"

"You'll have to tell me. I don't know."

"Why would I let him beat me up?"

"What better way to set up your alibi?"

Jack ate the last cracker, crumpled the cellophane wrapper, and tossed it in Desmond's wastebasket. He finished off the Pepsi and set the can on the desk so he could take it out to the recycle bin in the hall later. *What kind of killer would recycle aluminum cans?* he asked himself. He was sure Weems would have an answer for that, too.

"You should have been a cop," he told Sally.

"I'm sure you mean that in a good way."

"I do. Really. It's not just anybody who could come up with that line of reasoning."

"I've been teaching Poe."

Jack laughed. One of the things he enjoyed about Poe's detective stories was that the explanations for the crimes took up about two-thirds of the stories.

"I don't think these two murders are as complicated as what happened in the Rue Morgue," he said.

"Do you think they're related?"

"To the murders in the Rue Morgue?"

Sally just looked at him.

"I'm sorry. I told you I wasn't thinking straight. Anyway, this isn't Houston. We might be fifteen miles away, but we're still not a big city. So I think that when two guys connected with the college are murdered, the killings just about have to be related."

"You forgot to mention that both of the murdered men are connected with you, however tenuously."

"I didn't forget," Jack said. "And I'll bet Weems won't, either."

"Forget what?" Weems said, walking through the open door.

"I can't remember," Jack said.

15

It wasn't as bad as Sally had thought it would be. Weems led them through the events of the afternoon, listening carefully to everything they said and even agreeing that it would be stretching a point to ridiculous lengths to assume that Jack could have had any part in Thomas's death.

"It could even have been an accident," Weems said. "The back of Thomas's head was crushed. There was blood and brain matter on the floor, but we don't know yet how it happened."

Jack unconsciously wiped his hand on the leg of his pants. Weems didn't seem to notice.

"Maybe he tripped over his own feet somehow and fell in that grease pit," Weems continued. "It's a possibility."

"What about the man in the welder's mask?" Sally asked. "If it was just an accident, what was all that about?"

"How do you know it was a man?" Weems asked.

"We don't," Jack said. "But he, or she, was big, strong, and kicked like a mule on steroids."

"There are some big, strong women around," Weems said. Sally thought about Mae Wilkins, who wasn't big at all, though she might have been strong.

"Whoever it was walked like a man," she said. "And he had on men's pants and shoes."

Jack looked at her as if amazed at her powers of observation, which didn't surprise her. Men got distracted by little things like a welder's mask and didn't notice the important parts of a person's attire.

"Can you describe the shoes and pants?" Weems asked.

"The light wasn't good, but the shoes looked black, and so were the pants. I couldn't really tell much more about them."

"Have you told President Fieldstone about this?" Jack asked Weems.

Weems looked at him. "Not yet. We haven't been able to locate him."

Sally saw Jack glance at her out of the corners of his eyes. Everyone knew that Fieldstone made it a point of honor to stay at the college until five o'clock every Friday afternoon. But not today, apparently. Could he have been the man in the mask?

"Getting back to that accident theory," Sally said. "Why the mask?"

"If some guy just happened to be there when the accident happened," Weems said, "he might have had a reason for not wanting anybody to see him. Maybe he was afraid he'd be blamed for it."

"Surely not," Jack said. "He'd know that the Hughes police would never blame an innocent man for a crime."

Weems glared at him. "How are those ribs feeling? Still hurting?"

"Only when I laugh," Jack said. "Or breathe, or move."

Weems smiled. "I know what you mean. But in two or three months you'll be fine. More or less."

"Two or three months?"

"Well, you'll still have a little pain now and then, but three months is about right."

Jack sighed, which seemed to Sally to make Weems feel better.

"Can you think of anyone who might be afraid he'd be blamed for the accident?" Weems asked. "Somebody who might have a lot to lose?"

Sally thought of Jorge Rodriguez immediately, and she could tell that Jack was thinking the same thing. Maybe it was the remark about steroids that Jack had made.

And then she thought of Fieldstone. He would have as much to lose as Jorge if he was caught in a compromising position.

"I can't think of anybody," Jack said, with a glib nonchalance that Sally admired.

"Me neither," she said, though she wasn't sure she'd managed to be nearly as nonchalant as Jack.

"Okay, then," Weems said, seeming to accept their answers, "tell me this: Did Thomas know Ralph Bostic?"

"They were acquainted," Sally said. "Bostic wanted to eliminate all the college programs that weren't making money, and auto mechanics hasn't had great enrollments lately."

Weems looked at her thoughtfully. "So I guess if Bostic wanted to eliminate programs, he had plenty of enemies."

"More than one, anyway," Jack said. "You should've thought about that before you ran me in."

"I didn't run you in," Weems told him. "If I'd run you in, you'd still be in, believe me, probably becoming real good friends with some very strange people in the holding cell." Weems smiled, probably thinking of Jack in the holding cell, and then changed the subject. "What other programs did Bostic have it in for?"

Jack didn't say anything, and Weems looked at Sally, who looked at a photo of Eric Desmond receiving some kind of award from President Fieldstone. Maybe he'd been employee of the quarter or something like that. Sally couldn't recall.

"I can't hear you," Weems said.

"Only because we can't think of anything," Sally told him. "Auto mechanics was one program that Bostic had it in for, and I'm sure there were others. But English wasn't one of them, and as long as my department isn't threatened, I don't worry about it."

Sally really didn't feel that way at all, but she thought Weems would believe her. And maybe it would keep him from asking her anything else on the topic.

"Looking out for number one," Weems said.

"That's right," Jack said, following Sally's lead. "That's what the academic world is all about. Think about yourself and watch your back."

"Poor choice of words for an English teacher," Weems said. "The part about watching your back, I mean."

"I didn't mean it like that," Jack said. "Like Bostic. It's just that there are plenty of people who'll stick a figurative knife in your back around here if you're not careful. But not a real one. People in this profession don't much go for real knives."

Weems crossed his arms and smiled. "Another poor choice of words, I'd say, considering the knife that killed Bostic just happens to be yours."

Jack looked flustered. Sally felt a little sorry for him, but there was nothing she could do. He'd created his problem, and he'd have to solve it.

"You know what I mean," Jack said, which wasn't the most forceful of arguments.

Weems, however, surprised Sally by saying, "Yeah, I think I do. And I think you're not telling me all you know. But that's all right. I'll find out. And you can be sure I'll be keeping an eye on you while I do it. You're not out of the woods yet. You might not have killed Thomas, but that doesn't mean you aren't good for the Bostic deal. There's no way of getting around whose knife that was."

"You don't believe Jack killed anyone," Sally said. "You know that these two deaths have to be related somehow."

"You never know," Weems said.

"It would be too much of a coincidence if they weren't," Jack said. "We're not living in the murder capital of the world here."

"You should never underrate coincidence," Weems said. "I've seen a few that Charles Dickens would have been embarrassed to use."

"You know Dickens?" Jack said.

"That's right. *Beowulf* isn't the only thing I like to read."

"You read *Beowulf*?" Sally said.

"You think all I do is catch crooks?"

"No," Sally said. "I don't know why I should be surprised."

"Stereotyping," Weems said. "But I'm used to it."

"Stereotypes or not, I didn't kill Bostic," Jack said. "No matter how many coincidences you've seen or how many books you've read."

"I guess we'll find out about that, won't we," Weems said. He started out of the room, then turned around and came back in. "By the way, there's one other thing I meant to ask you."

Sally wondered if he'd been watching *Columbo* reruns. In between reading Dickens and *Beowulf*, of course.

"What's the other thing?" she asked.

"The lights in that auto shop. We couldn't get them turned on."

"Neither could we," Sally said.

"We finally had to get one of the maintenance crew to show us where the breaker box was," Weems said. "Somebody had tripped the switch."

"It wasn't us," Jack said.

"Assuming that you're telling the truth," Weems said, "and assuming that there really was someone else in there, whoever it was also knew where that breaker was."

"So?"

"So he was familiar with the building," Weems said. "Not just some guy who walked in off the street. You say you didn't know where the box was?"

Jack and Sally both nodded.

"Then he was even more familiar with the building than you are," Weems said. "That's something you might want to think about. I'll be seeing you around. Especially you, Neville. You might want to think some more about how your knife got from your desk to Bostic's back if you didn't put it there."

Weems gave a little wave. This time he went through the door and didn't come back.

16

Jack went home to take a nap and recuperate. Sally went back to her office because she needed a Hershey bar in the worst way. In fact, she couldn't think of a time when she'd been more in need of some chocolate comfort.

But she wasn't going to get it. When she reached her office, she was shocked to find two people waiting for her: Troy Beauchamp and Ellen Baldree. It was after five o'clock on a Friday afternoon. The campus should have been deserted. She didn't remember ever having seen anyone on campus at that time of day on a Friday. Of course, she usually wasn't there herself.

After about a second's consideration, however, Sally knew she shouldn't be surprised at Troy's appearance in her office. There wasn't much doubt that he was there to find out what he could about what had been happening. But Ellen was another matter.

"I was at the Seahorse Club, getting an early start on the weekend," Troy said. "I was just leaving when I saw the police cars heading out here to the campus. I thought I'd come by and find out what was happening, and someone told me that you were involved. Naturally I had to find out how you were doing, so I just waited for you in case you came back by your office."

"I appreciate your concern," Sally said, knowing full well that Troy was much more interested in getting the lowdown on what had happened than he was in how Sally was doing. "And you, Ellen?"

Ellen Baldree was perpetually unhappy with Sally for reasons that Sally had never quite been able to determine. She thought that probably Ellen would have disliked anyone in the chair's position, maybe because she wanted the job herself (though in Sally's opinion she was temperamentally unsuited for it) or maybe because she just didn't like to think that anyone was in charge of her. In her less agreeable moments, of which there were many, Ellen liked to remind Sally that she had outlasted three previous department chairs, the clear implication being that long after Sally was canned, Ellen would still be there at HCC, harassing the new chair and reminding her (or him) about the four that had come and gone while Ellen had persevered.

"It's a private matter," Ellen said, with a look at Troy, a look clearly designed to make Troy aware of how well she knew Troy would blab anything he heard to the first person he saw. "I've been waiting for quite a while, hoping you'd come back by, but I'd prefer to discuss it with you after Mr. Beauchamp is through."

"That's fine," Sally said. "You can wait in the hall. And close the door, please."

Ellen was clearly put out by having to wait, but she closed the door without slamming it.

"They didn't arrest Jack again, did they?" Troy asked when Ellen was safely out of sight.

"No," Sally said, and she told him as much as she thought he ought to know about what had happened.

"Good grief," Troy said when she was finished. "That must have been awful! And the police have no idea who's going around killing people?"

"None at all, if you don't count Jack."

"Surely they don't think he killed Ray Thomas, too."

"I don't believe they do, but it's hard to tell with Detective Weems."

"This is going to be hard on Mae," Troy said.

"Why on earth?"

"She and Ray were having a little fling. I thought everybody knew that."

"Not everybody," Sally said, wondering if Weems knew. And wondering if Troy, not to mention Weems, knew about Mae and Bostic.

"It's been going on for a while," Troy said. "I have no idea what she saw in him. He's as different from her as daylight is from dark."

Sally was about to say "opposites attract," but she stopped herself just in time. One use of that cliché a day was more than enough.

"Maybe she was getting free auto repair," she said.

"Maybe. But I still don't get it. He was in that shop all day, and when he left, he was so covered with oil and grease that he looked as if he'd been working on a drilling rig all day."

"I'm sure she made him clean up," Sally said.

Troy stood up. Sally could tell he was eager to get out and start spreading the news.

"We'll probably never know," he said. "I'm just glad you're all right, and I hope you won't let this upset you too much."

"Don't worry about me," Sally said. "I'm fine."

That wasn't strictly true. She didn't feel fine at all, mainly because there was something about the man in the welding mask that she'd told neither Jack nor Weems. But she couldn't let herself fret about that. She had Ellen Baldree to worry about first.

She thought about getting a Hershey bar from the bottom drawer of her desk, but she didn't want Ellen to see her eating it. Ellen would probably think it was a sign of weakness, and it might very well be. So Sally wasn't going to give her the satisfaction.

Ellen came into the office as soon as Troy slipped out the door. She'd obviously been lurking close by, perhaps in an attempt to overhear whatever was being said. She sat down by Sally's desk, crossed her legs, and said, "I want to know what you're going to do about Jack Neville."

Sally looked at Ellen. Her most striking feature was her hair, which was extremely black, as black as any hair that Sally had ever seen—which was surprising, given Ellen's age. She had to be at least fifty-five, and Sally refused to believe that anyone's hair could stay that black at that age, at least not without the help of chemicals.

But maybe she was being uncharitable, Sally thought. After all, her own hair was a constant trial to her. It reminded her of Shakespeare's sonnet, the one that went, "If hairs be wires, black wires grow upon her head." Not that the wires on her head were entirely black.

"Well?" Ellen said.

"I'm not sure what you mean," Sally said.

"Of course you don't. You don't know that Neville's your pet. You don't know that you have a date with him this weekend. You don't know, but everyone else at HCC does."

"And your point is?"

Ellen uncrossed her legs, sat up straight, and crossed her arms.

"My point is that you're the department chair. You aren't supposed to show favoritism. I'll be keeping an eye on the schedule for next semester, and if Neville gets an extra sophomore class or if he doesn't have to teach at eight o'clock, I'll complain to the dean."

"I make the schedule as fair as possible to everyone," Sally said.

"I'll bet. That's why Jason Kent's classes always fill up before anyone else's. We all know he's got the best schedule. Or he did. Now you'll probably fix things for your boyfriend."

Sally thought longingly of the Hershey bar lying quietly in the drawer not two feet from her. She thought of almonds and chocolate.

She also thought that Jason Kent's classes filled up because he was an excellent teacher who had remarkable rapport with his students. In her six years at HCC Sally had never had a complaint about any of his classes, unless you counted the woman who was convinced she should have made an A on the paper she'd cribbed from an article she'd located on the Internet. She'd explained to Sally that Mr. Kent simply didn't like her; otherwise he would have given her an A. After all, if the paper was good enough to be posted on the Internet, it was certainly good enough for an A at HCC. The fact that it was plagiarized in its entirety shouldn't enter into the discussion.

Sally didn't mention any of that to Ellen. She simply pointed out that Kent didn't always have a favorable schedule. Some of his classes were scheduled in the afternoons, and they always filled.

"No wonder they're filled," Ellen said. "There are hardly any other classes offered then."

"So what does that tell us?" Sally asked, expecting Ellen to say that nobody else would teach at those times because no one would sign up for their classes.

But Ellen fooled her. She said, "It tells us that he doesn't like competition. If there were any other classes, his wouldn't fill up."

"I don't think that's true at all," Sally said. "And by the way, Jack Neville is not my boyfriend."

"That's what I'd say, too, if I were going out with an accused killer. You'd better not let him back in the classroom. There are plenty of people who would take exception to being on the same faculty with him."

Sally counted silently to ten. Then she counted to ten again for good measure.

"For your information," she said when she was through with the counting, "the dean has already asked to teach Jack's classes for a while."

"I'm glad someone around here has a little sense," Ellen said.

"For your further information, I didn't agree with the dean's decision. I happen to believe that Jack is innocent. And even if he weren't, we should presume his innocence until he's been found guilty in court."

"They don't take innocent people in for questioning," Ellen said.

"I'm sure the people who wrote the constitution would disagree."

"They'd be wrong, then," Ellen said.

Sally had to admire Ellen for one reason if for no other. When she had an opinion, she stuck to it in the face of any and all opposition. Facts and reason meant nothing to her. She ignored them as blithely as if they didn't exist.

"Is that all you wanted to tell me?" Sally asked.

"Yes. And remember: I'll be having a very close look at the schedule when it comes out."

"I think that's an excellent idea," Sally told her. "Sometimes mistakes creep in, no matter how hard I work on it, so I'll tell Dean Naylor that you'll be double-checking everything."

"I didn't say that."

"And I know he'll appreciate your help," Sally said. "You know how he hates having errors in the schedule." Sally stood up. "I have to be leaving now."

Ellen stood as well, a look of surprise and shock replacing the determined glare she'd worn ever since sitting down.

"I didn't say I'd check the schedule for Dean Naylor! I didn't say anything about finding errors."

"He's always asking for more faculty input," Sally said. "He'll be thrilled to know that you'll be giving it to him."

"But I don't want to read the entire schedule!"

Sally put one gentle hand on Ellen's elbow and picked up her purse with the other. She guided Ellen toward the door and out into the hall.

"I'm sure Dean Naylor will be in touch," she said, pulling the door of the office closed behind her.

"But I don't want him to be in touch," Ellen said.

"Then you'd better tell him that you can't work on the schedule after all," Sally said, walking past her. "But he'll be disappointed if you don't. I'll see you on Monday."

"I don't know anything about checking the schedule," Ellen wailed behind her.

"That's all right," Sally said. "I'm sure you'll learn soon enough. Dean Naylor is a very good teacher. He's the one who taught me about making schedules. Of course you might want to give him some ideas for improvement."

Sally decided to leave it at that and walked away. She turned the corner into the main hallway and headed for the door. She could hear Ellen saying something, but it was muffled by the walls, and Sally didn't want to hear it anyway.

17

On her way out of the building, Sally stopped by the mail room. She wasn't really interested in picking up her mail. It was just that she was in the habit of checking it every day when she left. When she went in, Jorge Rodriguez was standing by his mailbox, removing one of the familiar brown envelopes used for campus mail.

"You're here awfully late," he said, looking Sally's way.

There was nothing in Sally's mailbox, and she was sorry she'd stopped by. There were two people she really didn't want to see at that moment. One of them was Fieldstone. The other was Jorge.

"I guess you know why," she said.

She didn't know exactly why she said it. She certainly hadn't intended to. Even if she'd wanted to discuss the topic with Jorge, she wouldn't ordinarily have put it that way. There was just something about him that flustered her.

Jorge didn't seem bothered. He stuck the envelope back in the box and said, "Why don't we go sit down in the lounge and have a talk."

Sally didn't want to go anywhere with Jorge, but it would have been rude to refuse. Sally usually tried not to be rude to anyone, something she blamed on her mother, who had spent a large part of Sally's childhood giving Sally detailed instructions about how a "lady" behaved. The only trouble with the instructions was that the world these days didn't have much use for the kind of women her mother had considered "ladies."

"All right," she said, telling herself that there was really nothing to worry about, even if Jorge was a killer. There might not be anyone around, but Jorge wouldn't try anything right there in the faculty lounge since anyone could walk in at any time, even on a Friday afternoon. "What did you want to talk about?"

Jorge didn't say anything. He just led the way into the adjoining room, which was furnished a little like a dentist's waiting room except that the magazines were older and more esoteric.

"Let's sit down," Jorge said.

Sally sat on the couch while Jorge sat in one of the forbidding chairs. Sally wasn't exactly uncomfortable at being alone with him, but she found herself thinking about the fact that Jorge had, after all, served time in prison for murder and that he might very well have been the person in the welding mask. She looked at his shoes. Black. And his pants. Black. He could have been the one, all right.

And then she found herself thinking about how attractive he was, prison record or no. She wished she hadn't stopped in the mail room.

"I know what you're thinking," Jorge said.

Sally sincerely hoped not. She smiled weakly and said, "And are you going to tell me what it is?"

"You're thinking that I'm a killer," Jorge said.

Sally tried not to look shocked, but she didn't quite succeed.

"And you're wondering about Ralph Bostic," Jorge said. "About whether I killed him or not. Probably everybody's wondering. Sure, I didn't like the guy. In fact, I thought he was a scumbag. He was ripping off the school, and at the same time he was posing as Mr. Fiscal Responsibility. I really can't stand people like that. I might be a lot of things, but I'm not a hypocrite."

Sally didn't know what to say to that, so she didn't say anything at all.

"You've heard the stories about why I was in prison, I guess," Jorge said.

Sally just nodded. One of the more popular renditions of Jorge's story had it that Jorge had come home from work early one day, caught his wife in bed with another man, and killed her lover with his bare hands. Sally didn't think much of that version. It wasn't that she didn't believe Jorge could do it. Just one look at his hands was all it had taken to convince her that it was all too possible. What she couldn't believe was that anyone married to Jorge would have to find another lover.

Another story was that Jorge had taken a baseball bat and beaten to death the man who had raped his sister. All things considered, that was the version that Sally preferred. It still wasn't pretty, but to her mind it portrayed Jorge as being at least as sinned against as much as sinning. Or something close to that.

Sally couldn't think of a way to put any of that into words, or at any rate, words that were appropriate to the situation, so she just said, "I've heard things, yes."

"I'll bet." Jorge grimaced. "Well, the truth of it doesn't matter much anymore. I did the crime, and I did the time, as we like to say in the joint. But the point is, I don't want to go back."

"And you're telling me this because . . . ?"

"Because I know you and Jack Neville have been talking to Weems. You know how I felt about Bostic, and I wouldn't want you to give Weems the wrong impression."

"What about Ray Thomas?" Sally asked. "How did you get along with him?"

"Ray? What's he got to do with this?"

He looked genuinely puzzled to Sally, but the people who taught in the prison units had a saying about the ability of inmates to fool people: *Why do you think they call them* cons? So maybe he wasn't as puzzled as he seemed.

"It's something I need to know," Sally said.

"All right, why not? Maybe you haven't heard the story, since it happened before you came here, but Ray and I had some trouble a few years ago. You couldn't say that we were friends."

"What kind of trouble?"

"He was teaching the automotive classes at the prison, and I found out that he was carrying in contraband."

Sally immediately thought of dope smuggled in boot heels, or stamps (as good as money in prison) concealed in hollowed-out paperback books, cigarettes (banned on all prison units) hidden in defective auto parts.

"What was he smuggling?" she asked.

"Candy bars."

Sally couldn't believe she'd heard correctly.

"Candy bars?" she said.

"That's right. He was taking them inside in his boots. He said he was eating them himself, on his breaks, but no one believed him. The wardens didn't trust him anymore, probably with good reason, so he lost his job in the prison."

"That doesn't seem like such a bad thing. He's teaching on campus now, so it's not like he was out of work, and the atmosphere is bound to be more pleasant."

"That's true, and it's also true that he has a good job, but he's not making as much money as he did in the prison. He was on a twelve-month contract there, but here he gets to work only nine months of the year. He doesn't have classes in the summer to make anything extra."

"And he blamed you for his losing the job?"

"That's right, and I don't mind taking credit for it. He broke the rules, and he got what he deserved. In fact, if I'd had my way, he wouldn't be teaching here at all."

"That all happened a long time ago," Sally said. "Does he still dislike you?"

"He's not the kind to forget."

"So have you seen him lately?"

"Not for a while. We don't socialize much. Why are you so interested in him?"

"Because somebody killed him this afternoon," Sally said.

Jorge looked taken aback, and Sally reminded herself that he might be feigning surprise for her benefit, though she didn't see how anyone could do such a good job of pretending.

"And you think I had something to do with it?" Jorge said.

"No," Sally said, hoping she sounded more convinced than she felt. "But I had to ask."

"I understand," Jorge said, but Sally could tell he was disappointed. She just hoped there was no sinister significance to his question.

He got up from the chair and moved over to the couch, taking a seat beside her. She didn't know whether to say something or to get up and move, so she did neither. Jorge looked at her earnestly with his big black eyes and took her hand in both of his. She felt her heartbeat accelerate, and she got very warm. She wondered if there might be some problem with the air conditioner.

"Sally," he said, "I have to tell you something."

Sally swallowed but couldn't speak, so she just nodded her assent.

"It's important to me that you realize my complete innocence in what happened to Ralph Bostic," Jorge said. "And I didn't even know about Thomas until you told me. Prison was in one way the best thing that ever happened to me, but I don't want to go back there, not ever, except as part of my job."

Sally swallowed and found that she could speak again. She said, "How could prison be the best thing that ever happened to anyone?"

"It's where I learned the value of education," Jorge said. "I dropped out of school as a kid because I didn't see any reason to keep going. I had friends, I had a job, so what did I need school for? It didn't mean a thing to me. And you know where that got me: right into prison. It was college that got me out. I got my GED, and then I started taking the HCC classes. I found out that I was pretty good when it came to doing things like working math problems and writing English papers. I found out I even liked those things. Too bad I didn't find out sooner. Anyway, you know the rest. I got my degrees, and I was a changed man. If everyone could have the chance I had, the prisons would be empty. And I want to help people see that. I can't do it if I'm back inside."

"But you didn't kill anyone," Sally said in what she hoped was a firm, confident voice, though she suspected it wasn't.

"Exactly," Jorge said. "But it might look suspicious to Weems that I had trouble with Bostic. And Thomas, too. I can't believe someone killed him."

"You can believe it," Sally said. "I saw him."

"I'm sure you did, but it's not easy to take it all in. Two deaths in one day. That's pretty scary."

If it scares you, Sally thought, *imagine how I feel.*

She didn't think it would be a good idea to say that, however, so she said, "What kind of job did you have before you went to prison? I know it must not have been in education."

"No," Jorge said. "It wasn't. It was nothing like that."

He stopped speaking and released Sally's hand, though she could still feel a bit of the heat.

"Well," she said, "what was it?"

"I was an auto mechanic," he said.

18

Sally had always thought Hughes was a pretty little town. It was located at the juncture of state highways 6 and 288, not too many miles from Houston in one direction and Galveston in another. It still had a small-town atmosphere, but that was changing. Developers had discovered that people would pay plenty for big houses only a short commute from Houston. Already houses were appearing everywhere, seemingly overnight, and it wouldn't be long before Hughes would become just another big, impersonal bedroom community.

Sally wasn't sure she liked what was happening, but there wasn't much she could do about it. When you lived near a place like Houston, change and growth were inevitable.

Sally even liked the hot, humid climate. It wasn't much good for manmade things, but it was certainly good for human skin. In the desert, skin dried out and wrinkled, but in the humidity associated with the Gulf Coast, skin stayed soft and pliable almost forever. Sally figured she was saving a fortune on moisturizers alone.

Plants loved the climate, too. Oleanders and crape myrtles blossomed with little encouragement and less care. Grass grew thickly on the lawns. Huge oak trees, some of which must have been at least a hundred years old, put out long branches that made a canopy over many of the streets. Of course now that Hughes was growing, the people who wanted to open new businesses or build new houses were cutting down as many of the trees as they possibly could, clearing land for parking lots and megastores, but it would be a while before all the trees were gone. There were too many of them, or at least so Sally hoped.

She drove down one of the oak-lined streets, thinking about Jorge. The fact that he'd been an auto mechanic was just a coincidence, she told herself, just like the fact that auto repair seemed to have so many connections to the two murders. Jorge had been so sincere about his innocence and his desire to stay out of prison that no one could have doubted him.

Well, Sally admitted, that probably wasn't true. Weems would doubt him. Weems doubted everyone as a professional habit. And Sally knew that she might very well be prejudiced in Jorge's favor, just because he was attractive to her. As much as she hated to admit it, she *was* attracted to him. It didn't seem right that she was, considering that he'd never showed the slightest interest in her, and especially considering that she more or less had a date with Jack Neville, whom some people were already calling her "boyfriend." What a stupid word. Jack was hardly a boy. But if you compared him to Jorge, she thought, the word didn't seem so stupid after all.

Sally looked up to see that she was just about to pass Mae Wilkins's house. There was another coincidence. Though it was possible to pass by Mae's house on her way home, Sally seldom went down this particular street, and she'd gone down it today for no reason that she could call to mind. Maybe it was her unconscious at work. Maybe she secretly wanted to stop by and have a little talk with Mae. After all, Mae was as likely a suspect in the murders as Jack. Mae had been having affairs with both the victims, if the gossip could be believed.

What if Mae had been having a third affair? Sally wondered. That would instantly create another suspect, someone jealous enough to eliminate the competition.

Sally pulled into Mae's driveway and parked her car beside a huge black Lincoln Navigator with an HCC parking sticker on the back window. The yard was perfect. The grass along the driveway was so evenly trimmed that it might have been cut with a pair of kitchen scissors. Oak trees, as perfectly trimmed in their own way as the edge of the lawn, shaded the yard, and not one blade of grass on the entire lawn dared to stick up higher than any other. There were gardenia bushes planted in front of the porch, and there was a flower bed where periwinkles and bluish-gray decorative cabbages grew. There was no grass growing in the beds, not so much as one stray sprig.

Sally got out of her car. There were no oil stains on the driveway and no dark mildew spots anywhere. Sally was almost embarrassed to walk on it with the same shoes she'd worn in the school's auto shop for fear of getting a spot on the virtually pristine concrete.

She walked on it anyway and went up to the front door, which might have been freshly painted only a week ago. The brass doorknob glistened like gold. The sound of the doorbell was a disappointment, however. It rang with only two tones, the traditional *bing-bong*. Sally was hoping for something more exotic.

Mae came to the door and opened it. Sally was shocked at her appearance. At school, Mae was never less than perfect, and as far as Sally knew not a hair on Mae's head had ever been out of place.

That wasn't the case now. Mae's short blond hair was mussed, and there were dark circles under her eyes, which were red from crying. Her nose was red, too, and if she had been wearing makeup earlier, it was mostly gone now. She clutched a crumpled tissue in one hand.

"Sally?" she said. "How nice of you to come by. Please come in."

The words sounded like something being recited by a robot, but Mae, no matter what her feelings were, could never be less than polite. She stepped back from the door, holding it open for Sally.

The inside of the house was immaculate, as Sally had known it would be. The tile in the entrance hall was sparkling. The carpet in the den might never have been walked on except with bare feet. There were fresh pink-and-white miniature mums in a vase on the coffee table.

The only surprise was that Vera Vaughn was sitting on the couch. Sally hadn't expected anyone else to be there, especially not Vera, who was undoubtedly the owner of the Navigator in the driveway.

It was just the kind of vehicle Vera would drive—black, macho, and bigger than anything else on the road. The "mine is bigger than yours" syndrome, which Vera liked to prove wasn't the prerogative of men only.

Vera often dressed in full dominatrix mode: leather skirt, boots, and shirt. Today, however, possibly out of deference to Mae's grief, she was wearing jeans, white leather walking shoes, and a white cotton shirt. Probably Sally shouldn't have been surprised to see her there because Vera and Mae had shared an office in the beginning of their careers at HCC and had remained friends ever since.

"Please," Mae said to Sally. "Have a seat."

Sally said hello to Vera and sat in a comfortable upholstered chair that didn't seem ever to have been impressed by another human body. Mae sat on the couch beside Vera, leaning slightly forward, her clasped hands clutching the tissue and resting on her legs.

"I wanted to say how sorry I am about Ralph Bostic," Sally told her. "And Ray Thomas. I know they were . . . good friends of yours."

Mae sniffled and dabbed at her nose with the tissue.

"Thank you," she said. "It was good of you to come by. But how did you know I cared about them?"

Sally couldn't very well say that she knew because she'd been asking. So she said, "It's just something I'd heard around the college."

"I suppose it wasn't much of a secret," Mae said. "They were both wonderful men."

Everything that Sally had heard about Ralph Bostic argued that Mae was completely wrong about him. And Thomas hadn't exactly been a paragon of virtue, either, not according to Jorge. Vera clearly didn't agree with the statement, either, if her loud sniff of disapproval was any indication. But then Vera didn't approve of men in general. As far as she was concerned, Bostic and Thomas were typical examples of a generally bad lot.

"I know lots of people wouldn't see it that way," Mae went on. "I know Ralph and Ray didn't seem like anything special, but they were very interesting in their own ways."

Sally was dying to ask what those ways might be, but she didn't think it was any of her business. Mae, however, didn't seem to mind talking about it.

"They were tremendously sexy," she said. "I think men who work with their hands at some menial task are very hot, don't you?"

"Uh," Sally said. She'd never heard Mae talk like that before. Her visit was suddenly turning into an episode of *Ricki Lake*.

"Men are worthless manipulators, most of them," Vera said. "They use women for their own needs, and that's all there is to it. Bostic and Thomas were no better than the rest, and maybe a little bit worse."

"Well," Mae said, "it's not as if a woman doesn't have needs, too. There's only so much housecleaning a person can do."

"Hm," Sally said, thinking that if her house were as clean as Mae's, there wouldn't be any time at all left over for fooling around with one man, much less two of them.

"They were always a little grimy, too," Mae said. "I like that in a man. Don't you?"

"Ah," Sally said, wondering how Mae kept the place so clean if she was going out with two such grimy guys. She decided she really didn't want to see the bedroom.

"Actually, I don't much like grimy men at all," Vera said. "The world would be a better place without them."

Sally thought Vera had a real way with words. Mae was probably really glad she'd come by. What a comfort.

"Without men," Vera continued, "world peace wouldn't be just a dream. It would be a reality."

Sally wasn't so sure of that. There would still be women like Ellen Baldree around.

"I just can't believe they're gone," Mae said. "Both of them, just like that. It's almost too much."

She lifted up the crumpled tissue and started to sob into it. Vera didn't seem inclined to do anything, so Sally moved over onto the couch and put her arm around Mae.

"I'm sorry," Mae said after a few seconds. She took a deep breath and gathered herself. "I'm all right now."

"Are you sure?"

"Oh, yes. I really shouldn't let things affect me that way, but I'm quite a sentimental person in some ways."

"Sentiment is highly overrated," Vera said. "You need to get in touch with yourself and stop leaning on men. You have your own identity."

"It's not like I was still going with either Ralph or Ray," Mae said. "I actually hadn't seen either of them in a week or so."

"Good," Vera said.

Sally thought about asking why the breakups had occurred, but she didn't think she'd have to. The way Mae was going on, all Sally had to do was wait and Mae would fill her in.

Mae didn't disappoint her.

"I started seeing someone else," she said.

"Oh," Sally said.

"Yes. It's been a big help to know that I can count on him in times like this."

"You don't need him," Vera said. "You don't need any man. Be strong. Be a woman."

Sally had a frightening vision of Vera morphing into Helen Reddy and singing a verse or two of "I Am Woman, Hear Me Roar" or however the song went. She could almost hear the opening bars, and she shook her head slightly to clear it.

"Besides," Vera said, looking ostentatiously around the room, "I don't see any males around here offering support. If you have a new guy who's so sensitive to your needs, where is he?"

"I'm sure he'll be coming by later," Mae said. "He has some other things to take care of first. He has quite a few responsibilities at the college."

Fieldstone, Sally thought. *Good lord!*

"There are so many things to do at the prisons, you know," Mae said.

Jorge, Sally thought. *That son of a bitch!*

116

19

Sally turned into her own driveway with her left hand on the wheel while she licked chocolate off the fingers of her right hand, the one that had been holding the Hershey bar she had stopped to buy at the 24/7 Mart.

Sally had thought at one time that there was a church on every corner in Hughes, but that wasn't true. It *was* true, however, that every corner without a church was occupied by a convenience store. Sally hadn't necessarily considered that a good thing until about five minutes ago, when her Hershey craving completely overpowered her and she'd been compelled to stop and buy a giant-sized bar. It had cost nearly as much as a gallon of gas, but it had been much more satisfactory. Besides, she liked hearing the counter man say "Have a good 'un" in an accent that reminded her of Apu, who owns the Kwik-E-Mart on *The Simpsons*.

She punched her garage door opener, and the lightweight metal door squealed up, rocking a little from side to side. She either needed to have the door adjusted or the house leveled. She thought she'd wait a while to do either one. She wasn't in the right mood for home repair.

Driving into the garage, she noticed that her lawn wasn't nearly as neatly kept as Mae's. Maybe she should think about changing lawn services. There wasn't much she could do about the interior of the house, however. She kept that herself, and she knew for sure that it wasn't in anywhere near the immaculate condition that Mae's was. And it never would be.

Maybe that was what Jorge liked about Mae, Sally thought: neatness. After all, Mae had only a master's degree, while Sally had a doctorate. Not that degrees meant anything, really, and it was silly even to think in those terms, but still.

And it couldn't be age. Sally wasn't any older than Mae, either. Well, okay, maybe a year or so, but that was it. Certainly no more than that.

Of course Mae did have that neatly cut blond hair, the kind that just sort of fell into place when Mae shook her head, which Sally had to admit was kind of cute and with which Sally's hair just couldn't compete. Mae definitely had the edge when it came to hair, no question.

Not that any of that mattered. What Mae had most of all was availability, and that, Sally told herself, was the key.

Sally had held herself aloof from the faculty and staff at Hughes for various reasons of her own, not the least of which was that she had really loved Ron, her husband, and losing him had put her into a kind of shock from which she hadn't emerged until she'd already been at Hughes for at least a couple of years. By then it was too late to change the pattern, or so she'd convinced herself.

On the other hand, if availability was the thing, Vera was certainly available. As far as Sally knew, Vera wasn't seeing anyone, and she was really very attractive in a crude, World Wrestling Federation sort of way. Some men were attracted to that look, and it seemed to Sally that Jorge might be one of them. But that was stereotyping. What did she know about Jorge's taste? Besides, Vera went out of her way to present an image of invulnerability and to express her contempt for the opposite sex. That wasn't exactly the kind of behavior that encouraged men to make advances.

And what was she worrying about Jorge for, anyway? Sally asked herself. Jorge meant nothing to her. Oh, he was attractive, certainly, and maybe he seemed a bit dangerous, which made him something of a challenge, but Sally certainly had no claims on him. She was sort of involved with Jack Neville, anyway.

Nevertheless, it made her angry that Jorge was going with Mae Wilkins. Was it fair for Mae to have three men panting after her, while Sally had none? If you didn't count Jack, that is, and he wasn't exactly panting, now was he? Things might seem somewhat better if Jack had done any actual panting, even just a little bit.

Sally looked around the garage carefully before getting out of the car. Satisfied that no one was skulking there, she closed the garage door and went into the house through the interior door that led into the kitchen. As soon as she stepped inside, Lola, the Meanest Cat West of the Mississippi (and possibly east of the Mississippi as well; the jury was still out on that) careened into the room, sliding on the tile as she rounded the corner. She had a bit of trouble righting herself, having something of a weight problem, besides having considerable trouble in getting any traction on the hard, slick floor. When she finally came to a stop, she sat like the Buddha and regarded Sally with something akin to contempt.

The look didn't bother Sally, who was used to it. Lola was a calico, and someone had told Sally that calico cats often had bad dispositions. Sally didn't mind. Lola could be affectionate enough when she chose to be. She just didn't choose to be very often.

In any event, Sally was glad to see that cat, whose presence meant that there was no one lurking around inside the house. If there had been, Lola would have been nowhere to be seen. She might have a bad disposition, but she wasn't exactly brave. In fact, she was about as courageous as a cabbage. She was extremely distrustful of strangers, even when Sally was with them, and tended to hide under the bed when anyone except Sally was around.

"Hungry?" Sally asked the cat.

Lola, of course, didn't answer, but then she didn't need to. She was always hungry, as both of them well knew. Lola had been put on a strict diet by the vet after her last checkup, a move that had not improved Lola's disposition in the least. It hadn't helped much with her weight, either, but Sally thought she could detect a slight change for the better.

She opened the cabinet to get Lola a kitty treat. One treat a day was Lola's total allotment, and she looked forward to it with an almost unholy anticipation. Her tail switched rapidly from side to side as she watched Sally's every move.

Sally tossed the treat in Lola's general direction, and Lola jumped to the side, snatching it out of the air as gracefully as a cat her size could do anything.

"Good girl," Sally said, and bent down to rub her head.

Thanks to the kitty treat, Lola was now in what passed for a pleasant mood, and she suffered the rubbing with as good a nature as she possessed, even to the point of purring a bit.

Then Sally checked her answering machine for messages.

"You have one new message," the metallic voice informed her when she pressed the button. "I will play one new message."

"Hello, Sally." The digitized voice of Sally's mother. "I hope you'll give me a call and let me know what's going on there. I just saw the news on TV, and it's very frightening. I hope you aren't involved. You're usually home before five on Fridays, and since you aren't there I'm worried. Please give me a call."

Nancy Jan Walton spent too much time worrying about her daughter, or at least that was Sally's opinion. But maybe that's what parents did. Sally and Ron hadn't been able to have children (a fact about which Nancy often offered vocal regrets), so Sally wasn't entirely sure.

She picked up the phone to make the call, but then she thought better of it. There was something else she needed to take care of first.

She went into her bedroom and opened the dresser drawer where she kept her pistol. Where other women might have kept nightgowns or slinky underwear, Sally kept her plain undies and a gun.

Lola, having inhaled the kitty treat, followed Sally into the bedroom.

"Shoo," Sally said, looking back at the cat. "You don't need to see this."

Lola gave Sally a disgusted look, sat down, and refused to move. Sally shrugged.

"All right, then. You can stay. But don't come any closer."

She opened the drawer and removed the gun case, put it on top of the dresser, and opened it. The Ladysmith was a lethal but lovely piece of machinery, smelling of gun oil. Sally felt a little better knowing that the pistol was where it belonged, but it wasn't as lethal as it looked because it wasn't loaded. That would never do.

Lola lost interest in the proceedings, possibly because there didn't appear to be anything to eat forthcoming, and left the room. That was fine with Sally, who didn't think untrained cats should be around firearms in the first place.

Sally kept the .38 cartridges in a separate drawer. She got them out, liking the feel of them as she took them out of the box, and slipped four of them into the pistol's cylinder. Might as well leave the cylinder under the hammer empty, she thought. If four won't do the job, the job can't be done.

Sally closed the case on the now-loaded pistol but didn't put it back into the drawer. She went into the kitchen where she found Lola sitting impatiently, tail swishing back and forth on the tile floor.

"I know what you want," Sally said. "You want tuna. But you can't have any. You're on a diet, and you know it. It's your own fault for eating too much."

Sally told herself that she only imagined that Lola's glare intensified at the word *diet*.

"You know the rules," Sally said. "One cup of dry food a day. And that's it."

Lola looked back disdainfully at her food bowl, which was still more than half full of the healthy (not to mention high-priced) reduced-fat cat food that the vet had recommended. It promised a balanced meal with plenty of protein, a combination of flavors that any cat would love, vitamins, minerals, and an ingredient that contributed to balancing a cat's pH factor. Wonderful stuff.

Lola, however, was not impressed.

"Meow," she said, which of course was all she *could* say, but it was clear from her tone that what she actually meant was, "That crap bites the moose."

"It probably does," Sally agreed, "but if you weren't so greedy, you wouldn't have to eat it. For that matter, you don't have to eat it anyway if you don't want to. You don't have to eat at all."

Lola looked at her calmly, twitched her tail once more, then got up and marched to the food bowl. She looked at the food for a second or two, then looked back over her shoulder at Sally as if to say, "I'll eat it, but I'm not going to like it."

"Nobody says you have to like it," Sally told her. "You do as you please. It doesn't matter to me whether you eat it or not. I have to make a phone call."

As Sally picked up the telephone on the kitchen counter, she could hear the steady crunching of the dry food between Lola's teeth.

20

Jack Neville sat in his home office playing Freecell on his computer. He'd won sixteen games in a row. The Kingston Trio's double CD of the albums *At Large* and *Here We Go Again* was playing on the computer's sound system, and Jack was listening to the last track of the CD, "A Worried Man," which he'd always thought of as the quintessential Kingston Trio song and which seemed particularly appropriate to him at the moment. It wasn't so much that the words fit his current situation; in fact, since they involve a love triangle, or maybe it was a quadrangle, they didn't fit the situation at all.

But the title fit really well. If there was ever a worried man, it was Jack Neville.

He was worried about his ribs, which weren't really hurting all that much, but that was because during his visit to the ER, he'd been given some pills for the pain. When the effect of the pills wore off, he'd be hurting, all right. Weems had assured him of that. He had a prescription for more pills, of course, but he didn't like taking medication if he didn't have to. He'd wait and see what developed. Maybe aspirin would be enough to keep things manageable.

He was also worried about Weems, who still seemed to think Jack might have killed Ralph Bostic, though it should have been obvious to anyone that Jack had done no such thing. At least the detective didn't seem inclined to blame Jack for Ray Thomas's death. Or maybe he was just trying to lull Jack into a false sense of security before he pounced and sent Jack away to the Big House.

Jack wished that Dean Naylor had been around after the Thomas murder. It was possible that Naylor would have been more sensible than Weems. He might even have granted Jack the right to teach his own classes again.

That was a laugh. Naylor was afraid of even the slightest hint of impropriety, and murder was about as big an impropriety as there was. He'd heard of Thomas's murder by now, and he was undoubtedly going nuts. If he had his way, Jack would probably never get back into the classroom again. So naturally Jack was worried about that.

He was worried about Sally, too. He wondered if she thought less of him because he hadn't fought off the masked welder. It wasn't as if he hadn't tried. His ribs were proof enough of that. But Superman he wasn't. He wasn't even Batman, if it came right down to it. Or Robin. More like Alfred, the butler.

The Kingston Trio CD stopped, and Jack took it out of the slot and put in another one, the double album called *Make Way* and *Goin' Places*. Jack wished he were going places, but he wasn't, so he might as well try to do something about his situation. Maybe he could deal with it intellectually.

He got out a sheet of paper and wrote down the names of the people who knew about his knife being in his office: Fieldstone, Jorge, Mae Wilkins, Stanley Owens, Ray Thomas.

He stopped with the last name. Did Thomas really know? Yes, he hadn't liked Jack, but he'd asked him once if he'd ever finished the knife, and Jack had said it was in his office if Thomas ever wanted to stop by and see it. Thomas, of course, had never stopped by, but he'd known the knife was there.

So, Jack thought, suppose Thomas had killed Bostic and then . . . well, Jack didn't know what came then. Thomas was dead, but Jack didn't know the actual cause, and he didn't know Thomas's connection with Bostic. But he left Thomas's name on the list anyway.

There were other people he could have added, too. Jack's mother, for example. She knew the knife was there because Jack had told her. But she lived in Dallas, a good five-hour drive away, and she didn't know either Thomas or Bostic. It would take someone with Weems's mentality to suspect her of the murder, though she was even less likely to be guilty of something like that than Jack himself.

Motive, Jack thought. His mother didn't have a motive. Who did?

Fieldstone did. Bostic wanted him fired. That was no surprise. Bostic was cheating the school, and Fieldstone didn't want him on the board.

That reminded Jack to add Hal Kaul's name to his list of people who knew about the knife. Hal must have known about Bostic's deal to fix the school's vehicles, and he must have known about the exorbitant charges. Maybe they were in on it together and had a difference of opinion. Thieves fall out. Jack added Kaul to his list of people with a motive.

Mae? Lovers fall out about as often as thieves, or at least that was Jack's opinion. He'd had a falling out or two himself.

Roy Don Talon. He had a motive, Jack thought, but had he known about the knife? Probably not, but Jack put his name down on the "motive" list.

But even if all those people had a motive to kill Bostic, what was their connection with Thomas? As far as Jack knew, there were no connections. So how could he tie the two murders together? The answer was easy. He couldn't.

The Kingston Trio was singing a song called "Hangman," and Jack stopped the CD. He didn't like the subject matter, though it had never bothered him before. He was getting a bit touchy about executions.

He left his list in the office and went into the kitchen, where he fixed himself a grilled cheese sandwich. When he'd gotten sick as a kid, his mother had often made him grilled cheese sandwiches as a special treat, and they'd been his comfort food ever since. He liked them with plenty of butter on the toasted bread. They just weren't the same without it.

He ate the sandwich and drank a glass of Pepsi One while he thought about the murders. He couldn't think of anything else to add to his lists, but maybe Sally could. He could always call her and ask, but he didn't think bothering her at home would be a good idea. After all, it was his fault that she'd been chased around the auto mechanics building by a hammer-wielding masked man.

He was sure she must be having second thoughts about having accepted his invitation to go out. Not because of the murders, however, or the masked man. He wished it had been because of the murders. He could handle that. No, it was something more fundamental, some kind of basic uncertainty that she wanted to go out with him at all.

Or that's the way it appeared to Jack. But he was no expert on reading people, especially women. It was possible that he was wrong about the whole thing. He hoped so.

There was one way to find out, or to take a step toward finding out, and that was to call her, whether he thought it was a good idea or not.

He went back into his office and looked up Sally's number in the faculty directory that he kept on the desk. Then he picked up the phone and punched the number. And got a busy signal.

He wondered who she was talking to. Oh well, he could try again later. Right now, he thought he'd have another grilled cheese sandwich.

21

Sally loved her mother. She even liked visiting with her now and then. But she didn't particularly like talking with her on the telephone. Coming over the wires, her mother's voice always seemed to have a vaguely accusing tone, whether she meant to or not. Her voice seemed that way on a cell phone, too, so it wasn't just the wires. But Sally could have been imagining it.

"I don't see how you can keep getting mixed up in things like this," her mother said after Sally had filled her in on recent events. "It just doesn't seem right, somehow."

"I'm not 'mixed up' in anything," Sally said, trying to make light of things. "Nothing's happening here."

"That's not what the reporter was just saying on the news program I saw. She's the one they always send out to the tragedies. Do you know the one I mean?"

Sally knew which channel her mother always watched, and she knew exactly which reporter her mother was talking about, a young, diminutive blond woman with even worse hair than Sally's. Or maybe it wasn't really worse at all. Maybe the reporter just pulled it as close to her skull as possible and plastered it there to keep from looking too glamorous when she asked people how they felt on learning that a close relative had just been killed in a fiery freeway crash.

"Reporters always like to exaggerate things," Sally said. "They like a big story, and if they don't have one, they invent it."

"But she mentioned something about a man in a hockey mask, like that terrible movie."

"It was a welder's mask," Sally said. "And it wasn't anything at all like a movie."

Which was true. It had been much worse than a movie.

"I knew you were mixed up in it! You were in danger! I could feel it."

Sally's mother liked to believe that she had some sort of extra-sensory perception where her family was concerned. She claimed to have experienced a ghostly visit by her sister the night of her death, and to have heard her long-dead mother's spectral voice calling to her the night her father died. The fact that no one else in the family believed the stories didn't appear to discourage Sally's mother in the least. "I know what I know," she always said when challenged on the subject. It was hard to argue with a statement like that.

"I wasn't in any real danger," Sally said. "Jack Neville was there with me."

"They didn't mention either of you by name, but I knew it was you. Is Jack the nice young man you're going out with?"

"I haven't gone out with him yet, and *young* might be exaggerating a bit, but he's nice, yes, even though he's been accused of murder."

Sally's mother didn't appear to have noticed her daughter's last remark.

"I'm sure he was a big help," she said.

Not really, Sally thought. *But at least he tried.*

"I hope you'll have a good time with him when you do go out," her mother went on. "You need to get out and have a little fun. After all, it's been six years now."

She had been insisting that Sally get out and have a little fun for at least five and a half of those years. One thing about mothers, they never stopped caring about you.

"But if he's accused of murder," Sally's mother continued in a worried tone, proving that she'd been listening after all, "how nice can he be?"

"He didn't kill anyone," Sally said. "Trust me. I know him better than that."

"Just how well *do* you know him?"

First her mother wanted her to go out, and now she didn't. Not that Sally was surprised. Her mother was a firm believer in the Emersonian idea that a foolish consistency was the hobgoblin of little minds. Except that consistency didn't have to be foolish for her mother to have nothing to do with it.

"He's been a member of my department for six years now," Sally said. "Ever since I came here. I think I know him well enough."

"You can never be sure how well you know a person. That's what the neighbors always say when that reporter interviews someone who lives next door to a killer. 'We thought we knew him very well. He seemed like such a nice man.' That's what they always say."

Sally thought back over the conversation.

"I believe *you're* the one who said he was a nice man."

"Well, I hoped that he would be if he was going out with my daughter. Is he?"

"Is he what?"

"Nice."

"Yes," Sally said, suppressing a sigh. "I told you that. He's very nice." *Maybe too nice. Maybe that's why I'm having second thoughts. But is it possible for anyone to be too nice?*

"I hope he's not too nice," her mother said, as if she knew what Sally had been thinking. It was a trick at which she was all too good.

"Can anyone be too nice?" Sally asked. Might as well. Her mother probably knew she was thinking it.

"I don't think so. When you're young, maybe you need excitement, but after a certain age, you don't need excitement. You need nice."

Sally thought about Jorge, who seemed pretty exciting, and

wondered if maybe she hadn't reached "a certain age" yet. She tried not to think about it too hard. She didn't want her mother picking up on it.

"Mother knows best," Sally said.

"There's no need to use irony on me," her mother said.

First Jack, now her mother, Sally thought. Maybe she was becoming insensitive to irony.

"I was an English major, too, remember," her mother reminded her, as if she needed reminding.

Her mother had taught English in high school for thirty-five years, retiring only a year before Sally's father, who had been a chemistry teacher himself, died of a heart attack.

"I remember."

"Good. I *do* know best, and I think you should stay as far away from this excitement as you can. Will you promise?"

"I promise," Sally said, in a tone that she hoped was sincere and convincing.

"Fine. Call me tomorrow."

"I will," Sally said. "I love you."

"And I love you. Good-bye."

Sally hung up the phone. Lola, having satisfied her craving for food momentarily, was sitting at her feet, staring up at her.

"What are you looking at?" Sally said.

"Meow," Lola said.

"I promised I'd stay away from the excitement," Sally said. "What are you worried about? That something might happen to me and you'd starve to death?"

"Meow," Lola said.

"Well, don't worry about it. I'll be sure you have plenty of food. Besides, I meant what I said. I'm staying away from the excitment. I meant what I said."

"Meow," Lola said.

"I know what you mean," Sally said. "It's easy enough for me to promise to stay away from the excitement. But what if the excitement won't stay away from me? That's what I'm worried about."

"Meow," Lola said, looking smug.

"I don't have to worry about a thing, do I," Sally said. "Not with you to protect me."

Lola didn't dignify that remark with a comment. She strolled under the kitchen table, flopped down on her side, and started licking one of her front paws. After she had licked it a couple of times, she swiped it along the side of her nose. Then she started licking it again.

Sally watched her for a second, thinking about how single-mindedcats could be, and about what she might eat for supper. She looked out the kitchen window and noticed that the sun was going down. That wasn't good, and she tried to think about something else. She didn't want to worry about the excitement that might come looking for her but that she had promised to avoid.

The telephone rang.

Sally picked it up, thinking that her mother was calling back with some bit of advice that she'd forgotten to pass along the first time.

"Hello," she said.

There was no response.

"Hello?"

Nothing, not even heavy breathing.

"I have Caller ID," Sally lied, thinking that she should have subscribed to the service long ago.

Except that it wouldn't have mattered. The telephone company had made it easy to block Caller ID, probably at the request of thousands of companies engaged in telephone solicitation who knew that no one would pick up the phone if they knew that Frank's Timeshares was calling.

But Sally was relatively certain that this wasn't Frank's Time-shares on the line. She didn't bother saying hello again because she was sure she wouldn't get any response. She just hung up.

She looked down at the telephone for a few seconds, thinking that it might ring again. After a little while, she decided that it wouldn't, for which she was grateful.

There was one little thing she hadn't mentioned to her mother. She hadn't mentioned it to Weems or Jack, either. She'd tried not even to think about it, but she was thinking about it now.

She was still thinking about it, and about the pistol in the bedroom, when the telephone rang again.

22

Sally let it ring. She wasn't going to be harassed by a telephone, whatever else might happen. She waited to see if the caller would say anything when the answering machine picked up.

After four rings, she heard her own voice, or a reasonable facsimile, saying that she couldn't come to the phone right now but if the caller would please leave a message, she'd return the call as soon as she could.

"Sally?" Jack Neville said. "I didn't mean to bother you at home. I just thought—"

Sally picked up the receiver and said, "Hello, Jack. I was in the other room and couldn't get here before the machine picked up."

"Oh." Jack sounded relieved, as if he might have been afraid she wouldn't take his call. "I really hate to bother you at home. I know how I feel when students call me about business on the weekend."

"So this is about business?"

"Yes," Jack said. "Well, no. No, it's not really about business."

"Is it about the murders?"

"No," Jack said. "It's not about that, either."

Sally had things pretty well figured out at that point. She had a Ph.D., after all.

"I think we need to talk, Jack," she said, deciding to take the reins of the conversation. "Why don't you come over? On second thought, maybe I should come over there."

"You should?"

"I think it would be a good idea. How much time do you need?"

"Time?"

"To get ready for a visitor."

"Oh," Jack said. "Well, I wasn't really expecting anyone, and—"

"Don't worry. I'm not the world's greatest housekeeper, either. I'll be there in an hour."

"Do you know where I live?" Jack asked.

"I have your address, and this is a small town. I can find you."

"Okay," Jack said.

Actually it was an hour and five minutes before Sally arrived at Jack's house. She had taken time to have something to eat and to take a shower. Not that she was getting herself fixed up to see Jack. She just wanted to be comfortable. She wore a pair of faded jeans and an old cotton shirt.

Jack met her at the door. He was wearing jeans, too, and trying to look casual, but Sally could smell freshly applied aftershave, and his shirt looked suspiciously new. Either that, or it had been freshly ironed. Sally wondered how many men knew how to iron these days.

Sally carried her purse in her left hand. In her right was the rosewood case.

"What's that?" Jack asked, gesturing to the case.

"My gun."

Jack looked shocked and backed up a step.

"I promise that my intentions are honorable," he said.

Sally laughed. "I never doubted it. So are mine."

"Then why the heavy artillery?"

"It's not heavy artillery. It's a thirty-eight. Can I come in, or are you going to make me stand out here all night?"

"I'm sorry. Come on in. I was just a little surprised to see that you were carrying a gun. Are you afraid I'll try to stick a knife in you?"

"I think the only person in the department who'd like to do that is Ellen Baldree," Sally said, following Jack into his den.

It was an interesting room, mainly because it looked exactly like the kind of room people might think a bachelor English teacher would have. Floor-to-ceiling bookshelves filled one entire wall, and they were filled with books, some of which were lying on their sides in front of other books that were on the shelves behind them. Some of the books were hardbacks, some were paperbacks, and it was easy to see that they weren't there for decoration. There was also a large entertainment center with a TV set, a VCR, a DVD player, and a stereo system with racks full of CDs on both sides.

"I'm not much of a decorator," Jack said.

"It's a comfortable room," Sally said. "I'm sure it's filled with the things you like."

"Books, music, and old movies," Jack agreed. "Those are the things that I enjoy."

"You don't have a cat around? Or a dog?"

"No pets," Jack said. "Or animal companions, if you want to be politically correct."

"I'm not too worried about that. I just wondered if you liked animals."

Sally thought of Lola, who wouldn't care whether Jack liked her or not. She most assuredly wouldn't like Jack. She didn't like anyone, except possibly Sally, and she didn't like Sally all the time.

"Animals are fine," Jack said. "And maybe it's not true to say that I don't have a pet. I sort of have one."

"How can you 'sort of' have a pet?"

"I'm feeding a cat," Jack said. "It won't come in the house. It won't even let me get close to it. But it doesn't mind eating the food I put out."

"How do you know it doesn't belong to someone in the neighborhood?"

"It's a he, not an it. I've asked around. Nobody will claim him. You wouldn't blame them if you could see him, and he looks a lot better than he did when he showed up here. I think he'd been in a bad fight, or else he'd been run over by a car."

"You didn't take him to a vet?"

"I wasn't kidding when I said he wouldn't let me get close to him. Anyway, I put out some food and water for him, and he's been hanging around ever since. Now and then he goes off for a while, but he always comes back."

"What does he look like?"

"He's big and gray and a little ragged around the edges. Not as ragged as he was, though. If he ever gets tame, I'll take him in for a checkup."

"Good idea," Sally said.

There was a short, awkward pause.

"You can put the pistol anywhere," Jack said.

Sally put her purse and pistol case down on a battered old coffee table that looked as if Jack had found it at a garage sale. She had to move several magazines and a stack of student papers aside to make room. Sally didn't mind the clutter; in fact, she was glad to see it. She would have been depressed if Jack had been a better housekeeper than she was. She had been mildly pleased when she saw that his lawn wasn't as neat as Mae's.

There was a green pen lying by the papers. Sally picked it up and looked at it.

"I went to a workshop once," Jack said by way of explanation. "The speaker told us that students had been intimidated by red marks on their papers ever since they started going to school. She suggested that we try a different color. Frankly, I can't see that it helps."

Sally put the pen on top of the papers. Probably not many people would realize it, but English teachers had to do a lot of their grading at home. If they did a good job of keeping up with all the essays their students wrote, there was no way to do all the work during regular office hours. Even if you were practically accused of murder, you had to keep up.

"I was hoping to get those graded in time for Naylor to return them on Monday," Jack said. "Students expect instant feedback these days."

"I know what you mean," Sally said.

She picked up a couple of magazines. *Texas Monthly*. *National Geographic*. She laid them back on the table.

"I subscribe to too many magazines," Jack said. "I'm trying to cut down. Please. Have a seat."

Sally sat on the couch, which, like the coffee table, had seen better days.

"Can I get you something to drink?" Jack asked. "I don't have any wine, but I do have Jack Daniels. I could mix you something. Or I have Pepsi One. And water. Just tap water, none of the fancy stuff."

Sally could tell that Jack was feeling a bit awkward. He wasn't used to having people in his house.

"I'll take the Pepsi," Sally said.

Jack filled two glasses with ice and soda and set them on paper napkins on the coffee table. Then he sat at the end of the couch opposite Sally.

"You said you had something to talk about," Sally prompted him, picking up her glass.

"Uh, yes, but maybe you'd like to tell me about the pistol first."

Sally took a sip of her drink, then set the glass on the napkin.

"I got another phone call just before yours," she said.

"I called about a half hour earlier, but the line was busy," Jack said.

"That was my mother. This call came later, just before yours. I thought your call might be from the same person, calling me back."

"Who was it?"

"I don't know who it was."

"Man or woman?"

"I don't know that, either. Whoever it was didn't say anything."

"A breather?" Jack asked.

"No. Nothing like that."

"What was it then?"

"I think it was someone calling to see whether I was at home."

"And that's why the pistol?"

"That's why. Now tell me what you wanted to talk about."

"Wait a minute," Jack said. "I don't get it. Maybe I missed the punchline."

"You didn't have any way of knowing," Sally said, "so now I'm going to tell you."

Jack relaxed back against the couch and said, "Let's hear it."

"It's something that happened this afternoon," Sally told him. "I didn't tell Weems about it, either."

"He's not going to like that," Jack said.

"I don't plan on having him find out about it. There's no way he will unless you tell him."

"You don't have to worry about that. He and I don't confide in each other. So what happened?"

"You remember when the man in the iron mask was climbing out of the pit and I hit him in the head?"

"That wasn't an iron mask," Jack said.

"Literary allusion," Sally said. "Something every English teacher should know. Like irony."

"Irony?" Jack said.

"Never mind. Do you remember what I'm talking about?"

"I remember, all right. How could I forget? He fell back on top of me, and I hit my head on the floor."

Jack reached behind his head and felt the knot. It was still there, and still tender.

"I'm sorry," Sally said. "I should have asked about your ribs."

"They're fine," Jack said.

Sally looked doubtful.

"Okay, so they're not fine. But they'll be all right. I took some aspirin."

"I didn't know you were such a macho guy."

"I don't like painkillers. I have an addictive personality."

Sally waited to see if Jack would explain.

"Games," he said. "I like to play computer games. Hours on

end if I don't watch myself. It might translate to painkillers. But I think we're getting off the track here. You were going to tell me something."

"Yes. When you fell back down in that grease pit, the guy in the mask fell on top of you. The welding mask bounced up just a little."

"And you saw his face? You should have told Weems about that. There's no telling what he'll do when he finds out."

"He's not going to find out because it never happened," Sally said. "I mean it happened, but not the way you think. I didn't really see a thing."

"Why not?"

"Because it was dark and he was down at the bottom of the hole. And because the mask didn't really rise up enough to show me that much. He pulled it right back down."

"Let me see if I have this straight," Jack said. "You didn't see him, so now he's threatening you by making phone calls and not saying anything."

"It sounds silly when you put it that way," Sally said. "But it's not silly, and I'm going to tell you why."

"Good," Jack said, "because I don't see why anyone would be bothering you if you didn't see anything. It just doesn't make any sense to me. Now I know how some of my freshmen students must feel when I'm trying to explain where the comma belongs in a compound sentence."

"It's really very simple," Sally said.

And then the telephone rang.

23

Jack jumped about a foot.

Sally didn't seem surprised.

"Are you going to answer it?" she asked.

"Sure," Jack said, getting up and heading toward the kitchen.

"Do you have Caller ID?"

The phone rang again.

"Yes," Jack called when the ringing stopped. "It says 'unavailable.' "

"Why am I not surprised?" Sally said.

Jack picked up the phone.

"Hello?" he said.

There was no answer. Jack looked through the doorway into the den at Sally, who shrugged.

"Hello?" Jack said.

Still no answer. Jack hung up.

"See what I mean?" Sally said when Jack returned.

"Why call me? I didn't see him. After I banged my head on the concrete, I didn't see anything except for some funny white lights."

"There's probably a name for those."

"I don't know it, though, and I don't even care. What I want to know about is those phone calls."

"I can't tell you anything. I just had a premonition something like that phone call might happen if that guy wearing the mask thought I saw his face. That's what I was going to tell you. It doesn't really matter whether I saw him or not if he thinks I did."

"You should have told Weems. You could have asked for protection."

Sally laughed. "I have a picture of that happening."

Jack smiled ruefully. "You're right. Weems would think you were crazy. He probably doesn't believe in premonitions."

"I kind of thought I was crazy, too," Sally admitted. "My mother's the one who claims to have psychic powers. Everyone thinks she's a nut."

"Even you?"

"Even me, but only about the psychic powers. In other ways, she's as sane as can be. At least she doesn't go around carrying a pistol."

"The pistol seems like a good idea right now," Jack said. "Have you ever shot anyone?"

"No. Only targets. That's what the instructor in the concealed handgun class liked to talk about—the difference between shooting a target and shooting a person. As Mark Twain said, it's like the difference between the lightning bug and the lightning."

"Twain was talking about choosing the right word when you're writing," Jack said. "Not shooting somebody."

"I think the analogy still works."

"We're only talking hypothetically here, though," Jack said. "We both know that you're not going to have to shoot anyone."

"I know that," Sally said. "And you know that." She looked into the kitchen at the telephone. "But does he know that?"

Jack looked worried.

"You sound almost as if you'd like to shoot him," he said.

"I don't want to shoot anyone. I'm not even sure I could. The instructor in the handgun class wasn't happy with me."

"It's a good thing there was no final exam."

"True. Anyway, now you know the situation. What are we going to do about it?"

"I'm not sure I do know the situation," Jack said. "You didn't come over here so I could protect you, did you?"

Sally smiled. "No. I'm the one with the pistol, remember? I think I just wanted some company."

"I'm glad you picked me, but maybe you picked the wrong guy. Now the man in the iron mask is calling me. If he's really the one who called. We don't really know that."

"We don't know that he called me, either, but it's interesting that we both got phone calls from someone who wouldn't identify himself, don't you think?"

Jack nodded. "I guess so. I wonder why he called here. I didn't see him. Do you think he knows you're here?"

"He might. It would have been easy enough for him to follow me if he was keeping an eye on my house. But speaking of phone calls, you still haven't told me why you called me."

"Never mind that now," Jack said. He looked uneasy. "It's not important at all, considering everything else that's going on. Let's just forget about it. Now that you're here, maybe we can figure out something that will get us out of this mess. Let me get my list."

"List?" Sally said, but Jack was already on his way out of the room.

When he returned, he was holding a piece of paper in his hand. He walked to the couch and handed it to Sally.

"This is the list," he said. "I tried to write down all the people who knew about the knife in my office and who might have had a motive to kill Bostic."

Sally looked over the names Jack had written and said, "I don't see your name on here anywhere."

Jack sat on the couch. "You're getting as bad as Weems. I didn't kill anybody."

"I know, but you did have a motive. That spat you had with Bostic at the board meeting even made the newspaper."

"If you can call what we have here a newspaper," Jack said.

Sally thought he was being a bit unfair to the *Hughes Daily News*, though she had to admit that the paper's true reason for existence wasn't to publish the news but to sell advertising space. Perhaps for that reason, the paper's single reporter didn't lavish a great deal of attention on local events, or any events for that matter, with the result that stories were sometimes so difficult to decipher that many readers simply gave up in despair.

"You're just resentful because the story about your run-in was clearly understandable," she said.

Jack opened his mouth to say something, then closed it and remained silent.

"Well?" Sally said.

"You could be right. Even Weems had read the article. He mentioned it to me. I've often wondered why every sentence in that story was so amazingly clear and to the point. You have to admit that it's uncharacteristic."

"We have enough to worry about without taking on the prose style in the *Hughes Daily News*. Everyone in town, including Weems, knows that you more or less accused Bostic of being a crook."

"All right," Jack said, pulling a ballpoint pen from his pocket. "Let me have that list."

"There are some other things you should know before you write your name down," Sally said, and she told him about Mae Wilkins.

"She certainly gets around," Jack said. "I didn't even know that she was going with Thomas, much less Jorge."

"Me either," Sally said, trying not to sound bitter. "And there's another thing. Jorge used to work as an auto mechanic."

"I'd heard that. So what?"

"Think about it. Everything's connected. Bostic repairs cars. Thomas taught auto repair. Jorge worked as a mechanic."

"That's really stretching a point."

"Roy Don Talon," Sally said. "He's on your motive list. He sells cars. He's the one who got A. B. D. upset about Bostic in the first place. A. B. D. went to the faculty senate, which is why you went before the board in the first place. If you look at it that way, Talon is the one to blame for all your troubles."

"When it comes to stretching a point," Jack said, "you're an expert."

"I think we should talk to him," Sally said. "Point stretching or not. There are too many automobile connections here for us to ignore them. He must know something about this."

"What about Fieldstone?"

"If we have to, we'll talk to him. Bostic was trying to get him fired, after all. And nobody seemed able to locate him this afternoon."

"All right. When do we start?"

"How about now?"

"It's Friday night," Jack said.

"Don't give me any more of that 'I don't like to bother people at home on the weekends' stuff. This is too important for us to worry about something as petty as that."

"You're right. It's just that I really don't like to bother people—"

"I told you not to start that."

"Sorry. I can't seem to control myself. I must have some kind of phobia."

"Get over it," Sally said.

"I already have," Jack said, but Sally didn't believe him. "Are you ready?"

"I'm ready. I'll make the first call."

"Call? I thought we were going to see people."

"Why is it that men never like to use the telephone?" Sally asked. "Do they just like to do everything the hard way?"

"I like to look at people when I'm talking to them," Jack said. He sounded a bit defensive.

"In this case, we don't have to. It's the kind of investigation we can do on the telephone. It won't take as long that way."

"I'm willing to wait."

Sally went into the kitchen and looked around.

"Where's the phone book?" she called.

Jack came into the kitchen holding their glasses and napkins, which he set on the countertop.

"In here."

He pulled open a drawer and pulled out the very thin book, which he handed to Sally.

"Thanks," she said, flipping through it.

When she'd located the number, she handed the book back to Jack, who replaced it in the drawer as she was punching the number on the phone. It didn't take long for her to get a response.

"Eva?" she said. "This is Sally Good."

After the "I'm fine, and you?" small talk and some oohing and ahhing over the awful events of the afternoon, Sally got to the point.

"Can you tell me where the president was this afternoon? No one could find him to tell him what happened."

Eva was hesitant. "I really don't think I should say anything."

"It's okay," Sally assured her. "I'm not going to tell anyone else."

Jack waved at her and pointed at himself, but Sally ignored him.

"I'd just like to know for my own satisfaction," Sally said.

"All right," Eva said. "I'll tell you, but if Dr. Fieldstone ever finds out, he'll throttle me."

"I hope you don't mean that literally."

Eva laughed. "Of course not. But it's supposed to be a big secret. He only does it every now and then."

"Does what?"

"Slips away to a movie. You know how quiet it is here on Friday afternoons. Nothing ever happens. I've worked in this office for over fifteen years, and I can't remember a single important thing that's happened on a Friday afternoon."

"Not counting today," Sally said.

"Oh. I forgot. That was about the biggest thing that's ever happened here, period. And nobody was around."

Sally decided not to remind Eva that she and Jack had been around. Not to mention Ray Thomas.

She said, "You mentioned that Dr. Fieldstone slips away fairly often."

"No, not often. If I said that, I didn't mean it. He hardly ever does. More like once a semester. And then only if there's something he really, really wants to see. He always documents the time away from campus and counts it against his vacation days, too, so there's nothing at all wrong with it. It's just that he doesn't think it would look good if people knew he was going to a movie. He always drives into Houston, where nobody knows him."

"And that's where he was today."

"Yes. He always calls at least once to check in with me and make sure things are going smoothly."

"Did he call today?"

"Yes, but that was before I heard that Mr. Thomas was dead, so I couldn't tell him about it."

"I'm sure he knows by now," Sally said. "Thanks, Eva."

She hung up the phone and looked at Jack.

"That pretty much eliminates Fieldstone," she said. "He was at a movie."

"It could be a cover-up."

"I doubt it. Eva talked to him, and it seems to be something he does from time to time. We can forget about him for now, I think. Are you ready for Hal Kaul?"

"Are you going to phone him?"

"I think he's a much more likely suspect than Fieldstone. We'd better see him in person. Are you ready?"

"I've been ready ever since you suggested it."

"Then what are we waiting for?" Sally said, picking up her purse and pistol. "I'll drive."

24

They were almost at the front door when Sally stopped and said, "Did you hear a noise outside?"

"Probably just Hector," Jack said.

"Hector?"

"The cat I was telling you about. When he came here, I thought he looked a little like Hector must have looked after Achilles finished dragging him around the walls of Troy behind his chariot. So I named him Hector."

"And now he makes noises outside your house?"

"Sometimes. He sneaks around in the bushes hoping he can find a bird to pounce on. Or maybe a lizard. I have some kind of lizards around here. They're all over the place. They even get inside the house."

Sally didn't think the noise had been a cat chasing a lizard, but she couldn't be sure. Lola was strictly a house cat.

"Your car's in the garage," she said. "Maybe we should use it instead of mine."

"You think there's someone out there?"

"Maybe that's what the calls were about. Maybe he was checking up on us. Now that he knows we're together, he can get us both at once."

"You really have an odd way of looking at things," Jack said. "It's just the cat."

"All right, then, we'll go in my car. Hold my purse."

Sally handed her purse to Jack, who took it awkwardly. Men never seemed to have any idea of how to hold a purse. She took her pistol out of its case, then closed the case and handed that to Jack, too.

"I hope you're not going to shoot my cat," Jack said, eyeing the pistol.

"I'm not going to shoot anyone, I hope. But you know the Girl Scout motto: Be prepared."

"That's the Boy Scout motto."

"Whatever. It's a good motto, no matter who thought of it."

Sally held the pistol close to her chest, her finger alongside the trigger guard.

"Open the door," she said.

"I thought you were supposed to jump through the door, stick the gun straight out in front of you, and hold it with both hands," Jack said. "That's the way they do it on *Nash Bridges*."

"This isn't TV," Sally said. "The firearms instructor for the handgun class told us that if you tried something like that in real life, the bad guy, assuming there's one out there, would just grab your arm and take your gun away from you. And probably break your finger if you have it stuck through the trigger guard. If you hold the pistol close like this, with your finger along the side, it's a lot harder for anyone to get hold of it, and the gun is a lot less likely to go off by accident."

"Oh," Jack said. "Well, I admire your professionalism, but I don't think there's anything to worry about."

"We'll find out, won't we," Sally said. "Open the door."

Jack opened the door and gave it a push. Sally stepped through, and the warm, humid night air fit itself around her like a damp glove. It was very dark.

"What happened to your streetlight?" she asked.

"I don't know," Jack said. "It goes off all the time. I'll turn on the porch light."

"No!" Sally said. "If you do, we'll be silhouetted. Perfect targets."

"I'm beginning to think you're taking this seriously."

"Of course I am. Bostic and Thomas are dead, aren't they? You can't get much more serious than that."

"Maybe we should go in my car," Jack said.

"Too late. We're already out here. Close the door."

Jack closed the door and stepped out onto the front walk with Sally.

"Now what?" he said.

"We get in my car and drive away," Sally said. "Come on."

Jack followed her toward the little Integra.

"Remember those stories that came out around Christmas last year?" he said. "The ones about the guy who was supposedly going around to shopping malls and hiding under cars? When you got to your car, he'd slide out from under it and slice your Achilles tendon with a razor blade."

"Jack! Stop that!"

"It wasn't true," Jack said. "It was just some stupid urban legend. There's not room under a car for anyone to hide these days. They're too close to the ground."

"It makes me uncomfortable to hear that kind of story. Just for that you'll have to look under the car."

"I have broken ribs."

"Don't argue."

Jack, moving very slowly and carefully, got down on one knee and looked beneath Sally's car.

"I can't see anything under there. It's too dark."

"Then you'll just have to get in first. But be careful when you open the door. The interior light will come on, and you'll be—"

"Silhouetted," Jack said, slowly getting to his feet. "A perfect target."

"You catch on fast. But there's an upside."

"What would that be?"

"Maybe you'll be falling down because someone's cut your Achilles tendon. That way whoever shoots at you will miss."

"Some see the glass as half full," Jack said. "Others see it as half empty."

"Right. Now get in."

Jack reached out for the door handle, and something reached out from under the car and grabbed his ankle.

"Arrgghhh!" Jack said, jumping up and then falling backward as the sharp pain stabbed him in the vicinity of his Achilles tendon.

When he hit the ground, his head bumped the grass, aggravating the knot that was already there, and the pain from his ribs shot through him. He screamed even louder.

"Where is he?" Sally yelled. "I can't see him!"

"Don't shoot!" Jack said as Hector ran across his chest and streaked across the lawn. "It's only the cat!"

Sally walked over to where Jack lay in the damp grass beside the driveway with her purse and pistol case nearby.

"You scared me half to death," she said.

"You think you were scared?" Jack said. "I thought for a second someone had severed my Achilles tendon."

"Serves you right. Can you get up?"

"I'm not sure. I think I'll just lie here for a while. Look up at the stars."

"You can't see any stars. It's too cloudy and there's too much light from Houston anyway."

"Are you sure about that?"

"I'm sure. If you're seeing anything at all, it's those little white lights you told me about."

"Maybe you're right. I think the back of my head hit the ground. It doesn't feel so good."

"No wonder." Sally reached down with her left hand. "Let me help you up."

"Are you supposed to move an injured person?"

"I don't think you're injured, not any more than you were before. I know your ribs must hurt, but you can't lie there all night."

"It's my lawn. I can lie here if I want to."

"True, but the neighbors would probably complain." She thrust her hand at him. "Grab hold."

Jack gripped her hand, and she pulled him into a sitting position.

"That wasn't so bad, was it?" she said.

Jack moaned. "I think a dentist said that to me once."

Sally still had hold of his hand, and she gave an easy pull.

"Come on up," she said.

Jack got his feet under him and rose up off the ground with only a little bit of whimpering.

"If you hadn't told me that story about the shopping mall slicer, this would never have happened," Sally said.

"Sure, blame me. It was that stupid cat's fault."

"There's always a scapegoat handy," Sally said.

"Scapecat, in this case."

"Whatever. Do you think you can get in my car?"

"I'll try."

Sally opened the door, and Jack twisted himself into the seat without crying out. When he had his legs inside, Sally helped him with the seat belt, which was admittedly a bit hard to grab from the front seat without a great deal of bending. Jack clicked the belt closed, and Sally shut the door.

Jack sat there while she put her pistol back into its case and picked up her purse. When she got into the car, he said, "I told you there was nobody out here."

"You can never be too careful," Sally said, and started the engine.

25

Hal Kaul lived in one of the newest sections of Hughes, a monster housing addition called Horizon Ranch. It had sprung up practically overnight, complete with large, two-story houses, landscaping, an eighteen-hole golf course, and a number of small lakes.

"How can he afford a place like this?" Jack asked when they drove up. "The college must pay the business manager a lot more than the instructors get."

"Fair is fair," Sally said. "You know that colleges can get plenty of teachers. Where would we be without all those people willing to teach part-time for next to nothing? But a good business manager is a pearl of great price. One of those can save the school lots of money and manage what's there so that everybody comes out ahead."

"Right. That's the way it should work. So why is it that the business manager didn't blow the whistle on the school's deal with Bostic?"

Sally didn't respond. She parked in the driveway, and they got out. A couple of blocks away, more new houses were going up. The smell of new wood and sawdust filled the air.

Sally noticed that Kaul's lawn was much more impressive than either Jack's or Sally's, almost on a par with Mae's, though Sally was certain that Mae did all her own yard work, while Hal no doubt had a much more expensive lawn service than the one Sally used.

They walked up to the imposing front door, solid carved wood, and Jack rang the bell. Sally noted that the sound of the bell was much more satisfactory than Mae's. It had three different tones and a resonant *bong bing bong* sound. Actually, she thought, *bongs* one and three were the same, but it was still very nice, sort of like the NBC chimes.

A woman opened the door. She was small, shorter than Sally, and round and soft, not at all like her husband, who was all angles and planes, though equally short. Sally introduced herself and Jack, and asked if they could see Hal.

"Of course," she said. "Come on in."

They stepped on the tiled floor of the entryway, and Mrs. Kaul led them to a small room that was outfitted as a home office. They could see Kaul seated at his computer desk, looking at a seventeen-inch monitor. Sally could smell the scent of a vanilla candle burning somewhere in the house.

"Hal's doing online auctions," Mrs. Kaul said. "I'll let him know you're here."

She went into the office and said something to her husband, who looked up from his monitor and saw them. He nodded to his wife, who told them to come on in. His wife drifted off to another room, where Sally could hear muffled voices coming from a TV set.

Sally looked around the office. Kaul had all sorts of junk stacked around: costume jewelry, old toys, old magazines, old catalogs, even old phone books.

"I do this for fun," Kaul said, waving a hand at the room in general. "It's a kind of hobby. I buy this stuff at garage sales and flea markets, and then I resell it at the online auctions. I don't make much money doing it, but I have a lot of fun."

"Seems as if it would take quite a bit of time," Jack said.

"Not really," Kaul said. "I take a picture of something with my digital camera, or I scan it if it's flat. Then I just upload the picture and a description, price it, and it's done. It just takes a few minutes. But I'll bet you didn't come here to talk about online auctions."

"No," Sally said. "We came to talk about Ralph Bostic."

Kaul ran his hand through his sparse gray hair, which was cut very short as if somehow to disguise the fact that there wasn't much of it.

"That's what I figured," he said. "Your friend Jack there is in a little trouble about that, from what I hear. Is that right, Jack?"

Jack acknowledged that it was.

"Glad to hear that the old school grapevine is still functioning as well as ever. You can always count on it. Now, what was it that you wanted to know about Bostic?"

Sally looked at Jack, who picked up his cue.

"You probably know I had a fracas with Bostic at a board meeting."

Kaul nodded.

"Well, it seemed to me that if Bostic was repairing cars for the school, someone knew how much it was costing. Someone should have caught on to the way the college was getting ripped off a long time ago."

"And I'll bet I know who you think that someone is," Kaul said.

"I'm not making any accusations," Jack said. "I was just wondering how things were handled. I know there are forms that have to be filled out, and I know that someone has to write the checks. All that stuff eventually has to cross your desk, I suppose."

"But you're not making any accusations," Kaul said, his voice dry.

"No, just wondering."

"Well, then, I'll set your mind at ease. Or maybe I'll just give you something else to worry about. You see, I did think those figures Bostic turned in were exorbitant. It took me a few months to catch on, but I did. And, like you, I wondered how he ever got the job of repairing school vehicles in the first place. You did wonder that, didn't you?"

"Yes," Jack said. "I did."

"And I'm just the guy who can tell you. The usual process is for us to develop a working relationship with a single garage for all our automotive repairs. They give us the best deal, and we give them all our business. Makes sense, right?"

Jack and Sally both nodded agreement.

"Sure it does," Kaul said. "So that's exactly what we did. For years, we sent all our work to Buddy Berry and everyone was happy. But let's say that even though you were perfectly satisfied with the arrangement you had, someone came to you, someone you trusted and thought would know all the angles, and told you that you could get a better deal somewhere else. What would you do?"

"The school's always trying to save money," Jack said. "I'd probably change garages, or at least have a look at what the better deal was."

"You wouldn't do it all that fast, though. You'd investigate things for yourself. You'd talk to the owner of the business, you'd get assurances that things would be even better than they'd been at Buddy's, you'd even check things out by sending a couple of vehicles over to the new place. Wouldn't you?"

"I guess so," Jack said.

"If you were going to do things right, you would. And that's what we did. Bostic was great, too. The repairs were done right, they were done fairly fast, and the price was fair."

"Then what about the figures I got?" Jack asked. "The ones that got Bostic so upset with me."

Kaul looked at his computer monitor and tapped a couple of keys on the keyboard.

"That all came along later," he said. "When it started, I took the bills to the person I trusted, the one who was supposed to be the expert, and had him check them out. He said they looked fine to him. He said we were getting a bargain."

"What about a conflict of interest?" Jack asked. "After all, Bostic was on the board."

"The vehicle repairs don't go out for bids, and Bostic just avoided voting on anything that seemed remotely connected to that kind of thing. So there wasn't any conflict. He was just a businessman, giving us a good deal. Or so he told us."

"That's interesting," Sally said. "But let's back up a little. Twice you've mentioned a 'trustworthy person' that you consulted. Are you planning to tell us who that person is?"

"Was," Kaul said. "I can tell you who he *was.*"

"All right," Sally said, surprised that a business manager would be so finicky about verb tense. "Who was he?"

"Ray Thomas," Kaul said. "That's who."

26

I told you it was about cars," Sally said.

"I guess you were right," Jack said.

Kaul said he wouldn't be at all surprised if she was, but that there was more to the story.

"Let us have it then," Jack said.

"Roy Don Talon's mixed up in it somehow," Kaul said.

"What about Jorge Rodriguez?" Sally asked, more or less hoping that Kaul wouldn't have an answer, or at least not one that would reflect poorly on Jorge.

Kaul's eyebrows went up.

"How did you know about him?" he asked.

Damn, Sally thought.

"Never mind how I know," Sally said. "It was more or less just a hunch, anyway. How is he involved?"

"I don't know for sure," Kaul said. "How about letting me tell this my own way?"

"Go ahead," Sally said. "I didn't mean to interrupt you."

"I'm not so sure about that. Anyway, Roy Don Talon's auto dealership is in some kind of trouble. It's all a little vague, just rumors so far, but something's going on there that's not on the up-and-up."

"Hey, I know that," Jack said. "Have you ever had any work done on your car at that dealership? You're lucky if your car survives. I had some windshield wiper blades installed on mine because they were an odd size, and I wanted to be sure it was done right. Two days later I was in a rainstorm in Houston, up on the Pierce Elevated, and as soon as I turned the wipers on, the blades just peeled right off. I thought I was going to die before I could get to an exit and get off the highway."

"I have to admit that Roy Don's repair department doesn't have a sterling reputation," Kaul said, "much less a commendable success rate, but that's not what the problem is."

"Then tell us what it is," Sally said.

"I told you that nobody knows for sure. There are just rumors that something's wrong and that Roy Don could be in big trouble. Money trouble. Lawsuit trouble."

"That sounds bad, all right," Jack said. "What does Jorge have to do with it?"

"That's a little mysterious, too." Kaul gave Sally a speculative look. "I thought I was the only one who knew. He came around asking me questions about Thomas, but he never would say why."

"Maybe it had something to do with Thomas losing his job at the prison," Sally suggested.

"I don't think so," Kaul said. "That was years ago. My conversation with Jorge was just last week."

Sally wished now that she hadn't asked about Jorge. It was beginning to seem more and more as if he might have something to do with Thomas's death. And maybe Bostic's, too.

"What about Fieldstone?" Jack asked. "Had he been told about all this?"

"He knew most of it," Kaul said. "If you hadn't nailed Bostic at that board meeting, Fieldstone would have. He was very upset with Bostic already because Bostic had accused him of fiscal irresponsibility, and when I told him what Bostic was doing to the college, he hit the roof."

Sally wasn't surprised to hear that. Fieldstone was rarely known to lose his temper, but when he did, no one wanted to be nearby.

Jack asked Kaul a few more questions, but he couldn't answer any of them. He seemed to want Sally and Jack to leave so he could get back to his auctions.

Sally took the hint, nudged Jack, and said, "We have to be going now, Hal. Thanks for your help."

Kaul started to get up, but Sally said, "Don't bother. We can find the door."

She took Jack's arm and guided him back outside. When the door had closed behind them, she said, "Could he have been lying?"

"Lying?" Jack said. "Why would he do that?"

"He could be the one who was conspiring with Bostic, not Thomas. Now that everything is about to come out into the open, he needed a scapegoat."

"Or a scapecat," Jack said.

"Stop that. This is serious business."

"Right. Scapegoat. But you're going to have to explain it to me. I don't get it. I must have missed something."

"Maybe you do have a concussion after all."

"I'm not seeing the little lights any more."

"Good. But you're not thinking straight, either."

"Oh, yes, I am. I can see what you're really worried about here. You're worried about Jorge."

Sally started to deny it, then stopped. After all, it was awfully close to being the truth. No matter how much she hated to admit it to herself, she was concerned about Jorge. She didn't want him to be a killer. Well, he was already a killer. She knew that. But that was different. She was sure of it.

"Let's get in the car," she said. "I could use some air-conditioning."

A breeze had come in off the Gulf, but it hadn't done much to lower either the temperature or the humidity, and Sally could feel her hair turning into a frizz that the Bride of Frankenstein would envy.

"Well?" Jack said when they were in the Acura.

"Of course I'm concerned about Jorge," Sally said, starting the engine. "He's a colleague, just like you are. I'm trying to help you, and I'd try to help him if he were falsely accused, too."

"Hmmm," Jack said as Sally backed into the street.

"And just what is that supposed to mean?" Sally asked.

"Nothing. I was just thinking. Let's get back to the scapegoat."

"Fine. Here's what I think. Maybe Hal knew he was going to be blamed for the cheating that went on in the billing. So he had to get rid of the two people who could fix the blame: Thomas and Bostic."

"That's not bad," Jack said. "And to make things even harder to figure out, he used my knife, knowing I'd get blamed, at least at first, because of my quarrel with Bostic."

"Right. So you agree that it could have happened that way?"

"Not really. There's too much it doesn't explain."

"Such as?"

"Jorge's involvement. And all that stuff about Roy Don Talon."

"What stuff? Hal didn't really know anything about Roy Don."

"Then I guess we'll have to find out," Jack said. "Won't we?"

"I suppose so," Sally said. "But not until tomorrow."

"I thought you didn't mind bothering people at home on Friday night."

"That was before I got tired," Sally said.

"Oh, Jack said.

Sally didn't want to visit Roy Don Talon, and she didn't want to talk about Jorge. What she really wanted was a Hershey bar.

"Do you eat candy?" she asked.

"Candy?" Jack said.

"That's right, candy. Like Hershey bars or Snickers."

"What does that have to do with anything?"

"Nothing. Just answer the question."

"I like Reese's Peanut Butter Cups," Jack said. "But I hardly ever eat them. I try to watch my weight." He looked at Sally. "But now might be a good time to have one."

"Good idea," Sally said.

She drove to the nearest 24/7 Mart and stopped the car.

"I'll be right back," she told Jack, and got out.

When she returned, she was carrying a Hershey bar and a package of two Reese's Peanut Butter Cups. She handed the Reese's to Jack and said, "My treat."

"Thanks. I didn't know you were hungry. I mean, we didn't have to get just a candy bar. I would've been glad to spring for a cheeseburger."

"I didn't want a cheeseburger," Sally said, unwrapping the Hershey bar.

They sat in the car and ate their candy, watching the customers come and go at the convenience store. Most of them appeared more interested in cigarettes, soft drinks, and lottery tickets than in food.

Jack finished eating first and crumpled the candy wrapper in his fist.

"Litter bag?" he said.

"Backseat."

Jack twisted himself around, and Sally could see that his ribs were hurting him. He dropped the wrapper in the litter bag and turned back.

"You should go home," Sally said. "You need to get some rest."

"I'm fine."

"No, you're not."

Sally folded the Hershey wrapper and deposited it in the litter bag. She resisted the urge to lick her fingers. She didn't think it would seem dignified. So she got a tissue from her purse and wiped her hands.

"Do you have any ideas about how to approach Roy Don Talon?" she asked when she was finished.

"Not a single one," Jack said. "Maybe we should just forget the whole thing."

Sally would have liked nothing better. It wasn't really any of her business. Except that Jack was a member of her department, and he was her friend. *Boyfriend* was too strong a word, but she did like Jack.

Besides, she was sure that Weems wasn't investigating properly.

If he were, he would have questioned Hal Kaul, and Hal would have mentioned it to them earlier. Weems must still think that Jack was somehow involved with the murders, or at least with Bostic's, and since Sally knew Jack was most definitely not involved, it was up to her, with Jack's help, of course, to prove it.

"I can't just forget it," she said. "Somehow I think we have all the pieces of the puzzle if we could just put them together in the right order."

"I keep thinking there's something I've missed," Jack said. "Some little something that would make a big difference if I could just think of what it is."

"Maybe that knock on the head made you forget."

"I don't think so. I think I'd already forgotten whatever it was before I got the knock. And the knot." Jack touched the back of his head. "I think the knot's getting smaller, though. Maybe I'll remember."

"Maybe what we need is a good night's sleep," Sally suggested. "We can go see Roy Don Talon first thing in the morning."

"Do you really think he'll tell us anything? If his business is in trouble, it's not likely that he's going to talk about it to the two of us. Besides, I don't think he likes you very much, not after that business about the picture."

"I'm sure he's forgotten all about that," Sally said, thinking of the painting that Talon had objected to and that had led to a lot of trouble for her and the college a while back. "It was just a simple misunderstanding. He was wrong, and I was right. He knows that, and he'll cooperate."

"I'll bet he will," Jack said.

"You should be more positive about things. Sometimes that helps."

"Easy for you to say. You're not the one Weems is going to put on death row."

"You're being overly dramatic again. You're not in any danger of going to prison."

"Tell that to Weems."

Sally thought about doing just that, and she realized that Jack had a point. Weems wouldn't listen. Which just proved her point. She and Jack had to find out the truth. If they could.

As her mother used to say, it was a mighty big *if*. She couldn't tell Jack that, however. She was the one who'd just told him to be positive.

So she said, "We'll probably figure it all out by morning. Talon might be the one with the key."

"I'll bet he will," Jack said again.

27

Jack sat on his couch drinking Pepsi One and feeling sorry for himself while listening to the Kingston Trio singing about how all their sorrows would be soon forgotten.

He should have known that things wouldn't work out between him and Sally, he thought. He hadn't had much personal experience along those lines, but he'd read more than enough books and seen more than enough movies to know that no matter what women said about liking nice, stable guys, when it came right down to it, they really preferred someone who walked a little bit on the wild and crazy side.

Jack wasn't wild, and he wasn't crazy. He was not Prince Hamlet, nor was he meant to be. He wasn't even meant to be Polonius. If he were going to fill a role, he'd probably be someone more like the comic sidekick in an old black-and-white western—Gabby Hayes, maybe, or Smiley Burnette.

Jorge, on the other hand, while he might not be Prince Hamlet, wasn't the sidekick type at all. He was Marlon Brando in *The Wild One*, or James Dean in anything.

Jack had never thought of Sally and Jorge as a couple, but it appeared that Sally had. Jack wondered if Jorge knew. He also wondered if Mae Wilkins knew.

Jack himself had never quite seen the attraction that Mae had for men. She was a little too neat for him, a little too precisely turned out. But it was clear that others didn't feel the same way at all.

The Kingston Trio had moved on to other songs like "Corey, Corey," all of which were considerably livelier than "All My Sorrows," and it lifted Jack's spirits a bit. To really feel sorry for himself, he needed some old-time country music, something by Webb Pierce or George Jones or Hank Williams. Senior, not Junior or the Third. Those guys were experts at self-pity, and a song like "He Stopped Loving Her Today" would probably have sent Jack so deep into the slough of despond that it would have taken him a week to climb out. Or maybe listening to the Kingston Trio sing "I Bawled" would have had him out in seconds. It was hard to be sad when you heard a song like that, even if the title sounded sad.

Jack decided to stop worrying about his virtually nonexistent love life and do something practical. He picked up his little list from the coffee table and tried to think back over everything he'd heard and seen that day. Surely somewhere in it there was a clue as to who had taken his knife and killed Ralph Bostic. He was sure of it. But the harder he thought about it, the less sense he could make of things, so finally he gave it up, took four aspirin, and went to bed, where he slept restlessly and dreamed of being pursued through the oak-lined streets of Hughes by a monstrous figure wearing a welder's mask. But instead of a ballpeen hammer the monster was carrying a knife of enormous size, swinging it within inches of Jack's fleeing figure and getting closer with every step.

The next morning Jack woke up feeling as if he hadn't slept at all. He was so tired that it was almost as if he'd actually been running from the swinging knife rather than sleeping and dreaming.

He got up, showered, and shaved. When he was dressed, he went outside and picked up the Houston *Chronicle* that lay at the end of the driveway. It was going to be a typical day in Hughes. The humidity was so high that Jack felt sheathed in sweat before he was back inside the house.

He sat at the table and read the paper while he ate his breakfast of dry cereal and skim milk. There was a short article about the murders in the metro section, but it didn't go into details, and it didn't mention Jack, at least not by name, for which he was thankful.

It did say, however, that the Hughes police were investigating every aspect of the case and that they had a "number of suspects."

"Sure they do," Jack said aloud. He thought he knew who the "suspects" were and that most of them were him.

After he finished his cereal, he went outside and put some food in a bowl for Hector, who was nowhere to be seen. He'd wander up later, when he got good and ready. Probably hiding under a car, waiting to sever the tendon of some unsuspecting soul, Jack thought. He changed Hector's water while he was at it, giving him some filtered water from the kitchen tap. Jack didn't think Hector cared about filtered water; in fact, he probably preferred water from some muddy puddle. But giving him the semipurified water made Jack feel better.

When Jack went back inside, the telephone was ringing. It was Sally.

"Are you ready to see Roy Don?" she asked.

"I guess so. If you're sure you want to."

"I do. I'll pick you up in ten minutes."

"I can drive."

"I know that. But your ribs will feel better if you don't."

Jack didn't argue. He sat on the couch and read the comics while he waited. He liked to start the day by finding out what Robotman was up to, though he identified considerably more strongly with Monty, Robotman's hapless human companion, unlucky in love and most other aspects of his life.

Jack heard Sally's car in the drive, so he dropped the newspaper on the couch and went out to meet her. He got into the little Acura without too much trouble. Maybe his ribs were getting better. Maybe Weems had been lying about how long it would take.

"Feeling better?" Sally asked.

"A little. Did you call Talon to let him know we were coming?"

"No. I thought it would be better to surprise him."

"I'm sure he likes surprises," Jack said.

Talon's automobile dealership was on the outside of town, down the highway toward Angleton. About six blocks from the dealership, the highway was dominated by a huge billboard that depicted Roy Don Talon, in full Roy Rogers regalia, riding atop a bucking automobile. He was waving his ten-gallon hat in one hand and hanging onto the reins with the other. The words TALON TAMES BIG CITY PRICES! were printed in large black letters above Talon's head.

"Very tasteful," Sally said.

"Very," Jack agreed. "And probably effective."

There were acres and acres of cars on the huge lot, since Talon had in some way or another captured a virtual monopoly on selling cars in Hughes. If you wanted a Toyota, Ford, Chevrolet, Chrysler, Cadillac, Oldsmobile, Jeep, Pontiac, Lincoln, or Mercury, you could find it at Talon's. If you didn't, you could drive to Houston or some other nearby town.

It was still early when they arrived at the dealership, but when Sally pulled into the gate at one end of the lot, they could see a double line of cars waiting to get accepted for service that day. Men with clipboards were going to each driver to ask about the problems with the car. When the work order was filled out, the driver would turn over the keys and wait for a ride back to town on the Talon Express, a shuttle bus that would drop people at their homes or at a store. Talon had only recently begun opening the repair service on Saturday, but it was clearly a big success. Jack couldn't understand why. After his experience with the wiper blades, he had found an independent mechanic he more or less trusted and had never gone back to the dealership.

"Isn't that Stanley Owens?" Sally asked.

Jack looked up toward the head of the line and saw Owens watching over all the action. When the cars were driven into the shop in back of the lot, the keys were brought to Owens, who took them inside his office and hung them on a rack, where they would stay until the work was done. Then the keys would be taken with the bill to the business office, where drivers could pay for their repairs, pick up their keys, and retrieve their cars.

"That's him," Jack said. "Maybe he could tell us what's going on out here. I know him a lot better than I know Talon. Of course you know Talon, so we can do whatever you think is best."

"Let's talk to both of them," Sally said. "Starting with Owens."

"Why not?" Jack said.

Sally parked the car away from the lines, and they got out. Owens was busy with keys and copies of repair invoices and didn't see them coming until they were fairly close. He smiled at Sally, and then seemed to notice Jack for the first time. His face changed, and for a moment Jack thought he might run.

I guess I'll have to get used to that reaction, Jack thought. *Nobody likes to see a suspected killer coming up to him early in the morning.*

Owens recovered quickly. He said, "Jack. It's good to see you. What can I do for you today?"

Jack introduced Sally and said, "We'd like to talk to you if you have a second or two. I'm in a little trouble, and maybe you could help me."

"I don't think so," Owens said. "I'm pretty busy, as you can see. I can't afford to stop now. The customers would never stand for it."

Jack started to tell him that the customers were plainly willing to stand for quite a lot if they were bringing their cars to Talon's for repair, but he didn't think that would be very diplomatic.

So he said, "I'd really appreciate it if you could give us just a minute. I promise we won't take too much of your time."

Owens looked extremely uncomfortable, but Jack hoped it was just the humidity, not the fact that Owens thought of Jack as a hardened murderer.

"All right," Owens said after a long pause. "Let me get someone to help out here."

He called over one of the men with a clipboard and asked him to take over for a few minutes. The man nodded and handed his clipboard to Owens.

"Let's go inside," Owens said, and he led the way into his long, narrow office, which had a window that looked out on the lines of cars. When he had closed the door, he put the clipboard on a long counter under the window and said, "Now, tell me what you want from me."

"We heard that there was some kind of trouble here at the dealership," Sally said. "We'd like to know what it is."

"I don't have any idea what you're talking about," Owens said. "This is one of the best dealerships in the state. There aren't any problems here."

"We're not talking about your repair department," Jack said. "It has to do with something else."

He was about to go on when the man who was taking Owens's place brought in some keys and invoices. He gave them to Owens, who made sure the keys were with the right papers.

"Now," Owens said, turning back to Jack when he was finished, "what were you saying about trouble?"

"Just that there's a rumor going around that Roy Don Talon's in financial trouble and might get sued."

"That's just a lie. Some of the big-city dealers don't like Roy Don, and they start rumors like that, hoping they can get some of our business. It happens all the time."

Owens was looking at the floor while he talked, and Jack didn't believe a word he was saying.

"Come on," Jack said. "Give me a break. I'm in serious trouble with the police, and I need something to help me get out of it."

"Even if Roy Don's business was in trouble, it wouldn't help you any," Owens said. "You have big-time problems of your own. They don't have anything to do with us."

"We don't know that," Sally said. "It could all be tied together somehow. That's why Jack needs your help. You were his teacher, after all."

"I didn't teach him to take a knife he made in my class and stick it in somebody's back," Owens said. "If I'd known what he'd do, I'd've never let him near me."

The assistant came back in with some more keys, and after Owens took them, he said, "I have to get back to work. We're swamped here today. You two should just go home."

He followed his helper outside. Jack looked at Sally, who was staring thoughtfully at Owens's back.

"He wasn't much help," Jack said. "I don't think Talon will tell us anything, either."

"You never know," Sally said.

"Positive attitude," Jack said. "I forgot."

"Don't forget it again," Sally told him.

28

There were three large buildings in the Talon Auto Complex, and Roy Don's office was located in the one in the center. When Jack opened the big glass door of the building, he felt a blast of frigid air that might have come direct from the North Pole.

"He must have the air conditioner set on *stun*," Jack said.

"It feels just fine to me," Sally said as they walked past the salesmen sitting at desks in their cubicles while they smoked filtered cigarettes and worked the phones with prospects they hoped to talk into buying cars similar to those sitting on the showroom floor, a bright red Toyota Celica and an equally shiny blue Corolla. The whole place smelled faintly of cigarette smoke and strongly of new rubber tires, leather upholstery, and whatever else made up that indefinable but highly seductive new-car smell. Jack felt an urge to get behind the wheel of the Celica and take off right through the plate-glass window and keep on going down the highway until somebody caught him. But he was in enough trouble already.

There was a semicircular counter in the middle of the large showroom, and a secretary sat behind it at a desk and switchboard. Before Jack and Sally could get to the secretary, however, they were accosted by a young man with slicked-back hair, tiny gold-rimmed oval glasses, a goatee, and a wide smile that was as bright as the cars. In a voice dripping with sincerity, he informed them that his name was Larry Hensley and that he was there to help them find the car of their dreams. Just exactly what were they interested in?

"We don't want a car," Jack said. "We're here to see Mr. Talon."

Larry's face changed. The smile disappeared, and when he spoke his voice had lost ninety percent of its sincerity. If he couldn't sell them a car, Jack thought, they might as well be a homeless couple who'd just come in from living in a culvert under the highway, for all the consideration Larry would give them.

"Mr. Talon's office is back down that hall," Larry said, nodding to a doorway on the far side of the semicircular counter.

"Thanks," Jack said, but Larry had already turned away, headed back to his cubicle.

"Nice guy," Jack said.

"Reminds me of a college administrator I once knew," Sally said. "No one at Hughes, of course."

"Of course," Jack said.

They walked up to the counter and got a brilliant smile from the secretary. Jack wondered if everyone who worked for Talon had naturally white teeth or whether they'd all had laser work done on them.

"How may I help you?" she said.

Jack looked at Sally. He could tell that she was as impressed with the *may* as he was.

"We're here to see Mr. Talon," he said.

"Do you have an appointment?"

"No," Jack said. "But I think he'll see us. Just tell him it's two teachers from the college."

"Oh," the woman said. "I thought I recognized you. You're Mr. Neville."

"That's right," Jack said. She looked vaguely familiar, but he couldn't place her. "Were you in one of my classes?"

"It was three years ago," she said. "My name's Jennie Fredrick. I had you for composition my first semester. You liked my paper on 'A Rose for Emily.' "

"I remember," Jack said, and he did. He had a better memory

for good essays than he did for faces. "You made the only A in the class."

"I was so happy with that grade," Jennie said. "I was afraid I wouldn't do well in college, but after that A I knew I was going to be all right."

Jack felt a warm glow, not because of anything he'd done, but because Jennie was a reminder of one of the good things about being a community college teacher. A lot of students came and went, and sometimes they went before their first semester had hardly begun, never to be seen again. But sometimes they stuck around, even the ones who were doubtful at first, the ones who would have been lost at a big state university, and they found out that they could do the work. Not only could they do it, but they could do it well. All they needed was a chance.

"I'm going to graduate in the spring," Jennie said. "Then I'm going to the University of Houston."

"That's great," Jack said, meaning it. "I'm sure you'll do well."

"I am, too," Jennie said. "I'll tell Mr. Talon that you're here."

She said something into the mike of a headset so tiny that Jack hadn't really noticed it until that moment.

"You can go on back," she said to Jack and Sally after getting some instructions through the headset. "It's the last door on the left."

"Success story," Sally said as they walked down the hall. "Makes you feel good, doesn't it?"

"It does," Jack said. "It also makes me feel bad that I won't be in class on Monday. I guess Jennie hasn't heard the news about me yet."

"What kind of positive attitude is that?" Sally asked.

"I keep forgetting."

"I told you not to do that."

"I'll do better," Jack lied.

"Anyway," Sally said, "your name wasn't mentioned in the paper. There's no reason for Jennie to know you're in trouble."

"She'll find out soon enough," Jack said, opening the door into Roy Don Talon's office.

It swung back to reveal Roy Don Talon himself, seated behind a desk about the size of one of the New England states. He was wearing a bone-colored Stetson and a jacket that reminded Jack of something Buck Owens might have chosen from his wardrobe during the glory days of *Hee-Haw* to go with his red, white, and blue guitar. When Talon saw Jack and Sally, he stood up and came around the desk, his right hand extended.

"Glad to see you," he said, offering his hand to Jack. "You, too, little lady. Dr. Good, right?"

Jack admired Sally's self-control as she said, "Yes, and you already know Jack Neville."

"Recognized his face from somewhere, and I figured it was the college," Talon said. Then he paused, and his face darkened as he stared at Jack. "Wait a minute. You're the son of a bitch that caused all the trouble about Ralph Bostic. Pardon my French, little lady."

Sally's nostrils flared, and her eyes narrowed. Jack started to say something to her, but he didn't get the chance.

"I'm not little, I'm not a lady, and that's not French you're speaking," she told Talon. "For that matter, Jack isn't a son of a bitch. I'm not so sure about you."

Uh-oh, Jack thought.

"Well, hell, then I apologize for calling him one," Talon said. "But I remember that big fight at the board meeting."

"As I recall, you weren't too fond of Ralph Bostic yourself."

"He was a son of a bitch. Pardon my French. But that's no reason for some faculty member to attack him."

Sally didn't argue the point. She said, "Maybe not. Anyway, we're here to talk to you about Bostic."

Talon looked puzzled. He looked at Sally and then at Jack.

"I don't get it," he said. "Why talk to me about him?"

"We think you might be able to help us," Sally said.

"You don't think I killed Bostic, do you?"

Jack wasn't so sure, but it would never do to say so. He let Sally continue to do the talking.

"Of course not," she said. "But you might have some helpful information."

"I doubt that. Weems talked to me for an hour or so, and I have a couple of alibis that you couldn't break with a nine-pound hammer. But why don't we sit down if we're going to talk about it."

Talon went back behind his desk, and Jack and Sally sat in two red leather chairs that were more comfortable than they looked.

"About that alibi," Sally said.

"I'll be damned. Pardon my French. Or whatever. You *do* think I killed old Ralph."

"No," Jack said, though it wasn't entirely true. "We just want to hear your alibi."

"Sure you do. Don't blame you. The cops are likely to think you did it since you had that fight with him. Only natural to want to pin the blame on someone else."

"I'm not trying to pin the blame," Jack said.

"Sure you're not. Anyway, my wife and I were celebrating our anniversary up at Cafe Annie in Houston. We dropped a big wad of dough for the meal, and it's on a credit card. That's alibi number one. We eat up there every now and then, whenever there's a special occasion, and I'm a big tipper, so the waiter remembers me. That's number two. Rock solid."

So that was that, Jack thought, waiting for Sally to think of the next question.

"What about the trouble your dealership is in?" she asked.

Talon leaned back in his chair, looking a little more relaxed than he probably was.

"Trouble?" he said. "What kind of trouble?"

"Oh, you know," Sally said. "Money trouble, lawsuit trouble. That kind of trouble."

Talon leaned forward, resting his arms on the desk. He didn't look relaxed now, not at all.

"I don't know what you're talking about."

"I think you do," Sally said.

Jack thought so, too, but Talon wasn't talking. He just sat there staring at them. For some reason, Jorge's name popped into Jack's head, and he said, "Do you know Jorge Rodriguez?"

Talon's head jerked. Jack could tell that he knew Jorge, all right. But Talon didn't admit a thing. What he said was, "Who the hell is that?"

"He heads up the college's prison program," Jack said. "I'm sure he's been at board meetings. He's probably addressed the board more than once."

"Oh," Talon said. "Him."

"Right," Jack said, not looking at Sally. "Him."

"Sure I know him. He's been around the board meetings. I've met him. What does he have to do with anything?"

Jack wished he knew. There must have been a reason he'd thought of Jorge, other than the fact that Sally was sitting there, but he couldn't think of what the reason might be. He also couldn't think of any reason why Jorge's name would upset Talon, but it did.

There was an uncomfortable silence that seemed to Jack to drag on long enough for glaciers to form and for one-celled animals to evolve into complex life forms. No one seemed to want to look at anyone else in the room.

Finally Sally said, "I don't suppose Mr. Rodriguez has anything to do with this. And it doesn't appear that you have any information that will help us."

She stood up, and Jack, figuring that they were throwing in the towel, stood up as well. He wondered if there was air-conditioning in prison, and if prison food was as bad as everyone said it was. He wondered how he'd adjust to steel toilets in the middle of the room. He wondered if he'd survive beyond the first week. Probably not.

"Thank you for seeing us," Sally said to Talon.

"My pleasure," Talon said, standing up behind his desk. He made no move to come around it and shake hands with Jack again, and it was clear that the meeting had been no pleasure for him, no matter what he said. "I wish I could help you, but you can see why I can't."

"Yes," Sally said. "But thanks anyway. Are you ready to go, Jack?"

Jack just nodded and followed Sally out into the hall. The door closed noiselessly behind them, but in Jack's imagination it clanged shut like one of the electric gates at the entrance to a prison unit. He wondered how he'd look in a white cotton uniform and how long it would be before someone beat him to a pulp or slipped a shiv between his ribs in the shower.

He wished again that he'd never signed up for that knife-making class.

29

As they walked back down the hall, Sally noticed that Jack's shoulders were slumped and there was no spring in his step. He was shuffling along like a man taking his final walk to the death chamber.

"Remember, Jack," she said. "Positive thinking."

Jack didn't raise his head or stop his shuffling.

"That's easy for you to say."

"It's easy only because I have a plan."

Jack didn't appear exactly ecstatic over her announcement, but he did stop and look at her.

"A plan?" he said

"That's right, a plan. We're going to find out what we came here for. Trust me."

"Right. Positive thinking." He tried a smile that didn't come off too well. "Just call me Mr. Jolly."

Sally didn't respond. When they reached the semicircular counter, she stopped.

"When's your break?" she asked Jennie.

Jennie looked at her watch.

"In about ten minutes," she said. "Why?"

"We'd like to talk to you if we could. Is there somewhere private we could go?"

"There's usually never anybody in the employees' lounge except me," Jennie said. "We could talk there. What would we talk about?"

"We'll tell you when you go on break," Sally said. "Come on, Jack."

She led him to a place where customers waited while salesmen "talked to the sales manager" to negotiate a better deal for them. In reality, Sally was sure that the salesmen and the manager didn't negotiate anything. Maybe they talked sports, or maybe they told jokes—probably many of them at the expense of anyone foolish enough to believe it was possible to get any kind of good deal when buying a car.

There was a low table with a few automotive magazines scattered on it, and the chairs weren't as comfortable as the ones in Talon's office, but Sally and Jack sat down anyway.

"What's the deal?" Jack asked morosely. He seemed to have forgotten that he was Mr. Jolly.

"The deal is that we're going to talk to Jennie," Sally said. "I should have thought of it sooner."

"Why her?" Jack asked.

"Why her? Who knows everything that goes on in any place of business? Who did we go to at the college when we wanted the down-and-dirty scoop?"

"Wynona," Jack said. Then it dawned on him. "The secretary."

"Right. I'll bet Jennie knows more gossip than anyone in this place. If we'd known you had a former student working here as a secretary, we could have saved ourselves a lot of time."

"But we didn't know," Jack pointed out.

"It doesn't matter. We know now. And she'll tell us what she knows because she likes you."

"I'm not sure that's ethical," Jack said.

"Ethical? You're worried about going to prison, and you're thinking about ethics?"

"I wasn't thinking," Jack said.

"Never mind. Of course it's ethical. Would it be any less ethical if she didn't like you?"

"I guess not."

"Then don't worry about it."

"I won't. And I'm sorry about bringing Jorge into this. I don't know why I did it."

"Don't worry about that either. I think you had a good reason."

"I wish you'd tell me what it is, then," Jack said.

Sally started to tell him, but Jennie came over and said she could go on her break. They followed her to the lounge, which happened to be on the same hall as Talon's office.

As Jennie had promised, there was no one in the room. It was furnished with a couch, a soft drink machine, a snack food machine, and a table covered with the same kind of magazines that had been on the table where Sally and Jack had been sitting, except that these were more recent issues. Someone had carved his initials in the tabletop.

"Anybody want a drink?" Jack asked. "Or a candy bar?"

Sally wondered if he was being a smart-aleck but decided he wasn't. Besides, she never turned down a Hershey bar. Unfortunately there wasn't one in the snack machine.

"They melt," Jack said when she mentioned it. "That's why you hardly ever see them in machines. How about some M&Ms?"

M&Ms were second best, but they would do in a pinch.

"And a Diet Coke," Sally said. "How about you, Jennie?"

"I'll have a Dr Pepper, thank you. No candy, though."

Jack bought some Reese's Peanut Butter Cups for himself and some M&Ms for Sally. Then he bought two Dr Peppers and a Diet Coke.

When everyone was settled and had managed to get the tops off their plastic bottles without spraying soda all over the room, Sally said, "Jennie, have you heard anything about Mr. Neville's trouble with the police?"

Jennie's eyes widened, and she put her Dr Pepper bottle down on the table.

"No," she said. "I hadn't heard anything like that."

Sally briefly outlined the situation, and Jennie's eyes got wider with each new revelation.

"Goodness," she said when Sally had finished. "There was something about Mr. Bostic on TV last night, but they didn't mention you, Mr. Neville."

"Which is a good thing," Jack said.

"I don't know why they suspect you, Mr. Neville," Jennie went on. "Anyone would know you'd never do something like that."

"Thanks, Jennie," Jack said. "It's too bad the police don't agree with you."

"You might be able to help us convince the police that they're wrong," Sally said, and asked Jennie if she knew about the problems at the dealership.

"Oh, sure," Jennie said. "We're not supposed to talk about it, though."

"In this case, I think you can make an exception."

Jennie took a swallow of her Dr Pepper and said, "Okay. I don't see what the big deal is, anyway. It's just as wrong to think Mr. Talon could do something dishonest as to think Mr. Neville could."

Sally popped a couple of M&Ms, blue and yellow. She didn't necessarily agree with Jennie's observation. She believed that car dealers would do just about anything for a buck, but this wasn't the time to go into that.

"Maybe telling us about the problems would help Mr. Talon, too," she said. "You never know what we might be able to do if someone will just give us the right information."

"I'll tell you, then," Jennie said. "It's something about stolen cars."

"Someone's been stealing cars from the dealership?" Jack asked.

"No, that's not it. Someone's been stealing our customers' cars from their homes. It took the police a long time to figure out that all the stolen cars were repaired at the same dealership, but they finally did. They haven't actually accused Mr. Talon of anything, but they've been pretty mean to him from what I've heard about it. They haven't found any of the cars, either. It's a big deal in

Houston, but there hasn't been much about it in the paper yet."

"Why is it a big deal in Houston?" Jack asked.

"That's where the cars are being stolen, mostly. Not many customers from here have had a problem."

"No wonder," Jack said. "Then the cops would have known that all the cars were from the same place. There isn't any other place."

"Lots of people buy cars in Houston," Jennie said. "Mr. Talon doesn't like it, but they do."

Sally nodded absently. Things were beginning to fall into place, though not the way she had hoped.

"Do you know Mr. Rodriguez?" she asked Jennie.

"From the college?"

"Yes. He's in charge of the prison programs."

"I never had him for a class or anything, but I know who he is."

"Have you ever seen him here at the dealership?"

"Once," Jennie said. "I work the late shift sometimes, and he was in here one night last week, just before everyone left. Everyone but Mr. Talon, that is. Sometimes he stays late, and Mr. Rodriguez came by to see him just before I went home. They were still in Mr. Talon's office when I left."

Sally finished the last of the M&Ms and drank the rest of her Diet Coke. She set the bottle on the table by the initials and said, "I guess that's what we wanted to know, Jennie. Thanks for your help."

"I hope you won't tell Mr. Talon that I talked to you about anything. He wouldn't appreciate it that I told you about the cars."

"We won't say a word. You don't have to worry about that. Are you ready, Jack?"

Jack was looking down at the initials on the desk. He put his bottle down and ran his finger over the carved letters.

"I don't know who did that," Jennie said. "It happened before I came to work here."

189

"I wasn't wondering who did it," Jack said. "I guess we should go now. Thanks, Jennie."

"I hope I've helped," Jennie said.

"You have," Sally said. "Believe me, you have."

"Good," Jennie said.

Sally wasn't so sure how good it was, not for Jorge and Talon. They were going to be the ones in trouble now.

30

A huge dark cloud had moved in from the Gulf while they were in the building, and by the time Jack and Sally were seated in her car, it had started to rain, big drops the size of dimes. They splatted on the windshield and thudded on the roof.

Sally had almost everything worked out in her head, or so she thought, though there were still a couple of loose ends. But something seemed to be worrying Jack, so she asked what it was.

"Those initials," Jack said, staring out at the rain. "Now I know what's been bothering me about the knife."

Sally started the car and turned on the air conditioner, though she was still cool from the potent arctic blast of the air conditioner in Talon's showroom building.

"So?" she said.

"When Weems took me to the police station, he said that my initials were on the knife handle. My initials are on there, but not my name. So how did he know it was my knife?"

"Was your middle initial on the handle?"

"Yes. It's K, by the way. For King. My mother's maiden name. Why?"

"Because Weems probably recognized the knife as being something that was made by hand. He must know about the knife-making class. How long do you think it would take him to find out how many faculty and students had the initials J. K. N.?"

"Oh," Jack said. "I thought it was probably a clue."

"It wasn't, I'm sorry to say."

"You sound as if you know something I don't know. What was all that about Jorge?"

Sally wasn't sure she was ready to talk about it. She said, "I'll tell you later. I have to think about it."

"Sometimes it helps to talk it out. Or write it down. That's what I tell my students. Writing is a form of thinking."

Sally wasn't in the mood for a composition lesson. She wanted to be alone, and she didn't want to talk.

"I'll have to think it all through before I write anything down," she said. "I'll take you home and give you a call this afternoon."

Jack didn't say anything more until they were at his house and Sally had stopped the car.

"I guess that means the date for tonight is off," he said.

"I think we should wait until a better time," Sally said. "Sometime when we don't have quite so many distractions."

Jack said he understood and got out of the car, wincing slightly.

"Take some aspirin," Sally told him.

"Thanks. I will."

He walked toward the door as fast as he could through the rain. He didn't look back, but at least he wasn't shuffling the way he'd been in the hallway at Talon's. Sally backed out of the driveway and went home.

Lola was waiting, bouncing around as if she were wired on caffeine.

"Calm down," Sally told her. "I'll get your treat."

When Sally tossed it, Lola made a grab for it as usual, but she missed. The treat bounced off her nose and skittered under the table, where it came to rest near a dust bunny. Lola eyed the dust bunny with suspicion.

"I'm not going to get the treat for you," Sally said, "and I'm not going to mop the floor. If you want to eat, you'll have to take the chance."

Lola overcame her hesitation and went after the treat, which disappeared into her mouth. The dust bunny, on the other hand, didn't disappear. Sally wished that it would.

She looked in the refrigerator for something to eat. There wasn't anything that looked particularly appetizing, but there was some pasta salad that she'd made with Tuna Helper a couple of nights earlier. That would have to do.

While Sally was eating, Lola hung around the chair winding herself in and out of the legs. Sally was sure that the odor of tuna was the reason rather than affection or desire for social interaction.

"Lola," she said, "you're a beautiful cat."

"Meow," Lola said, as if such self-evident facts didn't need stating.

"But you're not much help when it comes to solving mysteries."

"Meow," Lola said, looking up hopefully at the pasta salad.

"You're not getting any of it, so forget it," Sally told her.

Lola looked hurt. When that didn't work, she wandered off and flopped down in front of the refrigerator, where warm air came gently out of the vent. She began to groom herself, a process that Sally knew could take a long time, unless Lola was very sleepy, in which case it wouldn't take long at all.

Sally finished her salad and rinsed off the plate before sticking it in the dishwasher. She thought for a second about calling her mother, but she couldn't talk to her mother about any of the things she was thinking without going into a lengthy explanation.

So she went into her living area and lay down on the couch. She hadn't slept well, and she thought that a short nap would help her concentration. And sometimes in the past her unconscious mind had worked out problems while she was asleep, and when she woke up, she had the answers.

She drifted off to the sound of the rain on the roof, and soon she was dreaming. In the dream, she was climbing a high mountain, but instead of snow there was desert sand all around, and instead of cold there was heat. The higher she went, the hotter she became, and in the thin air she could hardly breathe. She gasped for breath, but she couldn't breathe in. It was as if some mighty weight were crushing her lungs.

She awoke with a start to find Lola lying on her chest and staring into her eyes.

"Lola!" she said. "Are you trying to suck my breath?"

"Meow," Lola said, implying that Sally should know better than to believe that old wives' tale.

Sally lifted Lola off her chest and set her on the floor.

"Maybe you weren't, then, but you're so heavy that you nearly crushed me."

"Meow," Lola said, highly insulted.

"I'm sorry," Sally told her. "I didn't mean that the way it sounded."

Lola sniffed and stalked away, heading back to the kitchen and her place by the refrigerator.

Sally ran a hand through her tangled hair and turned on the TV set. She found a cooking show and watched that for a few minutes. She was always intrigued by how easy it all seemed until she realized that the chef had everything prepared beforehand and even had a complete meal ready to show the viewers only seconds after sticking the dish in the oven. What took thirty minutes on TV must have taken hours in reality. It would have taken longer than that if Sally had been involved. She was definitely cooking-impaired.

She left the cooking show and surfed through the channels until she came to a movie made in the 1970s. All the men had bushy sideburns and wore bright paisley shirts with huge collars, along with bell-bottomed pants. The color was garish, and the overall look was cheesy. The look suited her mood, so she turned off the sound and tried to put everything she knew and surmised about the murders together in her head.

One of the things Wynona had mentioned was the rumor that Ralph Bostic had been involved in some scheme to steal cars and sell them in Mexico. Who better to work with in such a scheme than a car dealer? He would know what cars were available and where they were. Since he operated a dealership, he would have access to keys for every model he sold, and Roy Don Talon sold just about every model there was.

So, she thought, let's say that Talon and Bostic were working together. It seemed likely enough. But where did Ray Thomas come into the picture?

She thought about what she'd seen in the school's auto shop the previous afternoon, and about what she'd smelled. Fresh paint. And there had been a car there, all right. Suppose that Thomas was helping Talon and Bostic repaint the cars, maybe even doing some other kinds of things, like changing the engines? It made sense. Bostic was under suspicion, so he wouldn't do the work at his own shop. What better place to have it done than the college? No one would suspect that stolen cars were being repainted in a college auto shop.

Hal Kaul had strongly implied that Bostic and Thomas were working together to cheat the school out of money. Thomas was the one who'd recommended that Bostic repair the school vehicles. The stolen cars could be just another part of the deal.

Where did Jorge fit into all that? Sally was sure that Jack hadn't mentioned Jorge to Talon by accident. Whether he'd been aware of it or not, Jack had connected Jorge with the idea of problems at the dealership because Jorge knew about cars. He'd been a mechanic, after all. Besides that, he spoke fluent Spanish, and Wynona had said the stolen cars were being sold in Mexico. Jorge would have been the perfect middleman. His prison contacts might have been a consideration, too. Who could say what kind of people he'd met there and what they might be doing now? Maybe some of them were also involved.

Thomas had worked in the prison, too, of course, and he'd been forced to leave because he'd brought contraband onto a prison unit. It was possible, then, that he and Jorge had both made contact there with someone who'd helped set up the whole thing, from stealing the cars to selling them in Mexico. Bostic might not even have been the one behind the scheme. It could have been Jorge or Thomas.

And besides all that, Jorge would have been eliminating his rivals for Mae's affections.

Now that Sally had it all figured out, the question was, who had killed whom? If Fieldstone had found out that Thomas was running

195

stolen cars through one of the school's programs, maybe even using students to help, then Fieldstone couldn't be ruled out, not considering his temper. He might even have killed Bostic because of the way Bostic had been ripping off the college. The old alibi-by-phone trick had been used often enough in movies for Sally to know it could be discounted. It was hardly a reliable alibi in the cell phone era, after all. Fieldstone could have called from anywhere.

But what really worried Sally was the possibility that Fieldstone wasn't involved and that Jorge might have killed either Bostic or Thomas or both. If things had begun to unravel, and if Jorge had looked like a convenient scapegoat (*or scapecat*, she thought), which he certainly would have, given his history, then he might have decided to take care of his partners before they took care of him. He had been very impressive when he had talked to Sally about the fact that he was never going back to prison again, and she had gotten the idea that he would do whatever it took to remain in the free world. She wasn't sure if he would actually kill anyone, but, as people had pointed out, he'd done it before.

Still, even after all that, Sally somehow didn't think Jorge was guilty of anything at all.

To take her mind off things, Sally turned her attention to the TV set just in time to see a car crash through a roadside barrier and tumble down the side of a mountain, bursting into flames at the bottom. She was pretty sure the burning car wasn't the same model as the one that had shattered the barrier, not that she cared. A poorly executed car crash on TV couldn't distract her for long.

The trouble was that she didn't want Jorge to be guilty of anything, even if he was dating Mae Wilkins, and that was clouding her judgment. But if he wasn't guilty, how could she explain his late-night visit to Talon? She was convinced that there was nothing Talon wouldn't do. After all, he sold used cars.

On the other hand, maybe she was misjudging him. Maybe he was a completely honest man. It was just barely possible, she told herself, that she was stereotyping Talon based on nothing more than

196

hearsay. She'd come down hard on her students if they did something like that.

She told herself that she should call Jorge and talk to him, just come right out and ask what he'd been doing with Talon, but she couldn't bring herself to do it. She was afraid of what she might find out. Besides, if Jorge turned out to be guilty, he'd have to kill her.

Sally laughed aloud. The idea that Jorge would kill her was ludicrous. Jorge could never kill her, and he could never have killed Thomas or Bostic, either. Therefore someone else must have done it. Talon. Fieldstone. Or someone she hadn't considered yet.

She tried to think who that could be. An idea tried to nudge itself into her consciousness, but she couldn't quite dredge it up from the depths where it was hiding.

Then it came to her. Hal Kaul. Maybe that was what was bothering her—something about Hal.

What had Jack said when they drove up to Hal's house last night? It was something about Hal being paid a lot more than the instructors at the college. Sally knew that wasn't true, in spite of having joked with Jack about it. Kaul didn't make much more than she did.

So how did Hal get that big house on the golf course? Could he have been lying to her and Jack about things? What if Thomas hadn't recommended Bostic to him at all? What if Hal had been the one in league with Bostic instead? Jack's attack on Bostic at the board meeting would have made it clear that things couldn't continue as they had been, and Bostic could easily have threatened to make Hal the scapegoat (or cat, as the case may be).

Kaul knew about the knife, too. Framing the one who'd caused him so much trouble would be an excellent way to keep anyone from suspecting him.

Now that she thought of it, Sally wondered if Hal hadn't been just a little too glib, if he hadn't come up with his story about Thomas and Bostic just a little too easily. It would explain a lot.

Sally thought it might be time to pay Hal another little visit. But this time she was going to be very careful.

She turned off the TV set and went into the bedroom to get her pistol. It wasn't as if she could go into Hal's house brandishing a weapon, but she could keep it in her purse, just in case.

Lola stretched, got up from her comfortable spot in front of the refrigerator, and followed Sally into the bedroom.

"You can't go, Lola," Sally told her.

"Meow," Lola said, not seeming to care one way or the other.

Sally loaded the pistol and tried to put it in her purse, a hopeless task.

"One of these days I'm really going to have to clean this thing out," she said.

Lola meowed in agreement.

"Nobody asked you," Sally said, and started to remove used tissues, empty gum wrappers, various painkillers (aspirin, ibuprofen, Tylenol), nail files, a small bottle of hair spray (as if it would ever help), a roll of Tums, a calculator, four tubes of lipstick of various colors, and her cell phone.

Can't leave without the phone, she thought. She stuck it in the back pocket of her jeans. It wasn't comfortable, but that didn't matter. She could take it out and put it somewhere in the car.

"That ought to do it," she said, satisfied.

"Meow," Lola said in agreement.

Sally fit the pistol into the bag and hefted it, looking at herself in the pier mirror.

Not bad, she thought. Anyone seeing her carrying it might think that she just had a natural list to the right. Or to the left, if she switched hands.

"See you later, Lola," she said. Then she added, in her best John Wayne voice, which was none too good, "A woman's gotta do what a woman's gotta do."

"Meow," Lola said doubtfully.

"No, I'm not going to call Weems," Sally said. "He wouldn't listen."

"Meow," Lola said in agreement.

"I'm right about this," Sally said. "I know I am."

"Meow," Lola said.

31

―――――――

Jack wasn't hungry, but he told himself that he had to eat something. He was sure that he wasn't going to do well on prison food once he was locked up because he probably couldn't bring himself to eat it.

When he'd taught at the prison, which most of the HCC faculty had done at one time or another, he'd heard too many stories about the cooks spitting in the mashed potatoes, licking the meat after it was cooked, and a few considerably worse things that he didn't even like to think about, none of which contributed to a healthy appetite. Or to any appetite at all, for that matter.

He made himself a grilled cheese sandwich. Wouldn't be getting any of those when he was behind the twenty-foot fences topped with razor wire.

He ate the sandwich and went into his den. The house was cool, and he could hear the rain rushing off the roof. He wondered again about the air-conditioning in prison.

Of course the classrooms were air-conditioned. And he'd been to graduation several times in the chapel of one unit. The chapel wasn't exactly icy, like Talon's showroom, but it was acceptably cool.

Jack was pretty sure, however, that the cell blocks were cooled only by buzz fans, which didn't help at all in the summer when the temperature reached well into the nineties and sometimes into the hundreds on the outside. In the cells it would be even hotter, and the fans would just make things worse, moving the hot air around and practically cooking the inmates as if they were in a convection oven. Jack wasn't going to like that at all.

He shook himself and tried to laugh. He couldn't afford to spend the rest of the day sunk in self-pity. He knew that if he did, he'd never be able to put his mind to the things he should be concentrating on, like grading papers and trying to figure out who was really guilty of killing Ralph Bostic. It wouldn't do to worry about spending his life in prison, or the fact that Sally Good wouldn't go out with him.

After all, if he was going to spend the rest of his life in the Graybar Hilton, what difference did it make if Sally wouldn't go out with him? He'd probably be able to find plenty of dates behind bars. On the other hand, maybe not. He wasn't as young as he'd once been.

Stop it! he told himself. *That's not funny!*

To cheer himself up, Jack put Dolly Parton's bluegrass CD on the player. Sure, some of the songs on it were supposed to be sad, with titles like "Endless Stream of Tears," but Jack just couldn't be unhappy when he was listening to Dolly's clear soprano soaring over the banjos, mandolins, and fiddles. In fact, after only a couple of songs, he found himself smiling and humming along.

He got himself a glass of Pepsi One, put his feet up on the coffee table, and settled back to savor the songs. After listening to "Silver Dagger," he picked up his green pen and the student papers on the coffee table. He tried grading the one on top, but he couldn't get past the opening sentence: "I have read Flannery O'Connor's story in which I found it to be very interesting."

His put the papers back down, and his mind wandered. He found himself thinking of the murders and who might have committed them. He wondered what Weems was doing, not that it mattered. Weems was looking at the wrong suspects. Jack had one big advantage over Weems: Jack knew that he wasn't guilty.

But who *was* guilty? That was the big question.

Sally seemed to think she had some kind of idea, but she wouldn't tell him. Probably because it had to do with Jorge. That was just fine with Jack. He hoped Jorge was the killer. That would take care of the competition for life, because if Jorge went into prison again, he wouldn't be coming out, especially if he was guilty of murder.

The more Jack thought about that, however, the less he liked it. Sally might prefer Jorge to him, but that was no reason to want a guy to be stuck in prison for the rest of his life or, even worse, executed. And to tell the truth, Jack didn't really believe that Jorge was guilty. He'd worked with Jorge, and he liked him. It didn't matter that Jorge had once killed someone. Jack was convinced that had been a matter of sudden rage, or maybe it had even been justifiable homicide. Jack didn't know. No one did except Jorge, as far as Jack could determine. But that didn't really matter. Somehow Jack just couldn't see Jorge as someone who would kill Bostic and Thomas.

He tried sorting through everything he knew, or thought he knew. He'd heard what Sally had heard, so he should be able to reach the same conclusions she'd reached even if he didn't have a Ph.D.

But the more he thought about things, the less clear they seemed to him. It was too bad his hunch about the initials hadn't worked out.

On the other hand, maybe Sally had brushed off that idea all too quickly. True, Weems could have easily gotten copies of the rolls for the knife-making class, but what if he hadn't known the knife was handmade?

That wasn't possible, though. As much as Jack had admired his own craftsmanship, he knew he was nowhere near good enough to have made a knife that looked professionally constructed. There was a difference in a knife that was put together in a class by a first-time hobbyist and one that had been custom-made by an expert craftsman.

Weems had probably checked with the registrar, just as Sally had said, and that was that.

Thinking about the knife, however, gave Jack another idea. It hit him like a ballpeen hammer right between the eyes. He considered it carefully and turned it over and over in his mind. The more he thought about it, the more convinced he became that he was right.

When he looked at things in a certain way, everything fell into place. Oh, he didn't know the why of all the things that had happened, but he almost certainly knew who the killer was. It was so obvious that he wondered why it hadn't occurred to him sooner.

Jack went back over everything again. It still worked out the same way: One person he and Sally had talked to knew something he shouldn't have known.

People at the college knew what Jack had been accused of doing, or some of them did, but Jennie, who didn't work at the school, hadn't known anything at all about his involvement. Jack's name hadn't been in any of the newspaper articles, and it hadn't been mentioned on television. Sally had said something about that fact to him in the hall on the way to Talon's office. Even Talon hadn't known that Jack was a suspect, and Jack and Sally hadn't enlightened him. Talon was a board member. If anyone should have known, it was Talon.

So, Jack asked himself, how had Stanley Owens known?

Jack thought back over what Owens had said that morning. Something like, "I didn't teach you to make a knife just to stick it in someone's back."

He'd known, all right, and there was really only one way he could have known. He'd been the one who'd framed Jack. It would have been easy for him to get the knife and use it, as easy as it would have been for him to get keys to all the cars that had been stolen. After all, he'd have access to the drivers' addresses, right on those repair forms the drivers filled out every day of the week.

The stolen cars were the key to the whole thing, Jack thought. Bostic, Thomas, and Owens were working together, and when the cops closed in Owens had known about it just like everyone else at the dealership. He must have decided he didn't want to take the chance that either of his partners would give him up, so he'd taken care of them. He might even have tried to reason with Thomas, whose death could have been accidental. Maybe Owens had simply pushed him a little too hard and he'd stumbled backward into the grease pit. It didn't really matter how it had happened, though. Thomas was dead either way, and it was for sure that Bostic's death was no accident. Owens had put a knife in his back.

Jack was so excited by his discovery that he didn't know what to do next. He told himself to calm down and think things through. Easier said than done, but he finally got himself under control.

The logical thing to do would be to call Weems. Logical, but useless. Weems wouldn't listen. He'd accuse Jack of meddling, and then ignore him.

The most stupid thing to do would be to confront Owens personally.

"But I'm right about this," Jack said aloud. "I know I am. So confronting him wouldn't really be stupid. He'd have to admit what he'd done."

Jack looked at his watch. It was after one o'clock, and the so-called repair service at Talon's place shut down at noon. Owens might very well be at home already. Jack could look up his address and pay him a visit.

That's what he'd do, he thought. He wouldn't need any help, though it might have been a comfort to have Sally along for moral support. Well, moral support and firepower, since maybe he could have persuaded her to bring her pistol along.

Sally, however, had her own ideas about who was guilty, and she hadn't seen fit to share them with Jack. So why should he share his idea with her? After all, she didn't want to go out with him because she preferred Jorge, probably because she thought he was more of a man of action than Jack. Which he was. Or had been at one time.

But that was all in the past. This time, Jack was going to be the man of action. He was going to roust a killer, and he was going to do it alone. He'd prove to Sally that he didn't need any help. When it came to handling the Bad Guys, he could do just fine on his own.

Just like John Wayne.

And if that doesn't impress her, Jack thought, *nothing will.*

32

Sally took the cell phone out of her pocket, tossed it into the passenger seat, and pressed the garage-door opener. As the door rose, she looked into her rearview mirror and saw through the curtain of rain that someone seemed to have dropped a black mountain into her driveway, effectively blocking her exit from the garage.

On second glance, however, she saw that it wasn't a mountain at all. It was just Vera Vaughn's Navigator, which she'd probably bought at Roy Don Talon's dealership, unless she'd driven to Houston for the purchase. But she wouldn't have done that. All the college teachers bought their cars at Talon's. They didn't want a board member to think they were disloyal either to Talon or to the college district.

Sally wondered what Vera was doing there, and she wondered how Vera was going to let her know, since she had made no move to leave the Navigator, probably not wanting to get soaked by the rain.

The cell phone rang. Sally didn't have Caller ID on that phone, either, but she didn't need it. She knew who was making the call.

"Hello, Vera," she said.

"Hi," Vera said. "I was hoping we could talk. Are you about to leave?"

Sally resisted the urge to say that she hadn't been going anywhere and that she just liked to sit in her car in the garage and look out at the rain.

"Yes," she said. "But I can wait. What did you want to talk about?"

"In person," Vera said. "Not over the phone. You never know who's listening."

That was true, though Sally had no idea who would want to listen in on her cell-phone conversations, most of which were short, boring, and with her mother.

"We can go inside," she said.

"Fine," Vera agreed. "I'll just come in through the garage if it's all right with you. That way I won't get quite as wet."

"Okay," Sally said. "I'll leave the door up."

She turned off the phone and started to get out of the car just as Vera emerged from the Navigator. Then she had a terrible thought: What if Vera was the killer?

Sally couldn't think of any motive that Vera might have, though perhaps jealousy would do. There was Mae, getting all the men, and there was Vera, all alone. But Vera didn't seem to care about men, especially the grimy ones that Mae liked, so that couldn't be it.

Vera entered the garage, dressed in a sleek black outfit that looked as if it might be made entirely of rubber. Perfect for the weather, Sally thought, though it probably wasn't really rubber at all. On the other hand, with Vera you could never be sure. And it would probably be very easy to wash the blood off a rubber suit after you'd brained someone with a ballpeen hammer. Vera was big enough to have been the person Sally and Jack had encountered in the auto shop, and it wouldn't have been at all unusual for her to be wearing black pants and shoes that looked like men's footwear. For that matter, most women's shoes these days seemed to Sally to look as if they'd been designed for men. It was hard to tell the difference at a glance, or even on close inspection.

Sally told herself that she was being silly. Vera wasn't going to murder her in her own garage, not with her giant SUV parked outside for all the world to see. Though what with all the rain, no one was likely to notice it.

Sally reached in her purse, got out her pistol, and opened the car door.

"What's this all about?" she asked.

"It's Mae," Vera said. "I wanted to talk to you about something she said yesterday."

Now that Vera was practically next to the car, Sally could see that she wasn't holding a ballpeen hammer, or anything else. And the black suit, which was shedding water nicely, was just a Gore-Tex running outfit. Sally slipped the pistol back into her purse, hoping that Vera hadn't noticed it.

She got out of the car and said, "Let's go inside. We can have a cup of coffee or something."

"Great," Vera said.

They headed for the door, and Sally pulled a worn towel off a rack nearby. She liked to keep a few towels in the garage in case of emergencies.

"Dry yourself off if you'd like," she told Vera, who started patting herself down with the towel.

When she was mostly dry, Vera followed Sally into the house. Lola looked askance at the visitor, hissed once, and disappeared into the bedroom, where Sally knew she would hide under the bed until Vera was gone. And maybe longer.

Sally told Vera to have a seat and went into the kitchen. She put her purse on the counter, trying not to let it klunk. She opened the freezer, got out some coffee that she'd ground a couple of days earlier, and dumped it into the coffeemaker. She poured in some water and went to join Vera.

"It'll be ready in a minute," she said. "I hope you like hazelnut flavoring."

"That's fine," Vera said. "Do you believe in the social conventions, or may I be abrupt?"

Asking someone who was making coffee for a visitor whether she believed in social conventions was a little redundant, Sally thought, but she just said, "Be as abrupt as you care to."

"Good. I know people think I come on a little strong at times, but I can't help it. It's just my manner."

Sally thought about saying that no one thought that Vera came on a little strong. On the contrary, everyone thought she came on more powerfully than a locomotive. But Sally didn't think it would be wise to point that out.

So she said, "I don't mind."

"Then let's talk about Jorge Rodriguez."

Sally was sorry she'd said she didn't mind. The last person she wanted to talk about with Vera was Jorge.

"I think the coffee's done," she said, standing up and heading for the kitchen.

Vera followed her. Sally got two saucers down from the cabinet and set two cups in them. The coffee was ready, so she poured Vera a cup.

"Cream or sugar?"

Vera shook her head, so Sally poured her own coffee. She liked it black, too.

"Now, about Jorge," Vera said.

"Why don't we go back in the living room," Sally said, and she left the kitchen with Vera trailing along behind.

When they were seated again, Sally took a deep breath and said, "Now, tell me about Jorge."

"Mae thinks you like him," Vera said.

Sally took a sip of the coffee. It was still hotter than she liked it, but she pretended that it was just right. She swallowed and said, "I do. Everyone does."

"She thinks you like him in a sexual way."

"Oh," Sally said. "I see."

"No, you probably don't. You're not like Mae. She's the kind of woman who has to have a man around her, if you can believe that."

Sally could believe it.

"I've always admired you because you didn't seem to need

men," Vera said. "You seemed to be above that sort of thing. Then I heard about you and Jack, so I guess I was wrong."

"What about me and Jack?" Sally asked.

Vera sipped her coffee, then said, "That you were dating."

"That's not exactly true," Sally said.

"It's not? Everyone thinks it is."

"You know how gossip gets around a school. People repeat things just because they want them to be true."

"So," Vera said, "you're not going out with Jack?"

Sally wondered why her relationship with Jack was so interesting to Vera. She said, "We'd made some tentative plans. I'm sure that's how the rumor got started. Things didn't quite work out the way we thought they would, though."

"Because of Jorge?"

"I didn't say that."

"No, but Mae is very suspicious of you. She thinks you're scheming to take Jorge away from her."

"Nothing could be further from my mind," Sally said, knowing that she wasn't being exactly truthful.

Or maybe she was. Whatever her feelings for Jorge were, they didn't involve scheming.

"You want to know something?" she said.

"What?" Vera asked.

"This is as bad as eighth grade, huddling in the restroom and talking about boys. You'd think we'd have gotten beyond this sort of thing."

Vera blushed. Sally wouldn't have thought it possible if she hadn't seen it for herself.

"I know," Vera said. She stood up. "I'm sorry I bothered you. I think I'd better go."

She started for the door, and Sally had an inspiration. She didn't think Vera had come to talk about Jorge at all.

"Vera," she said, "have you got a crush on Jack Neville?"

Vera stiffened, stopped, and turned around.

"I wouldn't call it a crush," she said. "I don't know what it is, exactly. I don't know what's gotten into me. That's why I'm acting like a schoolgirl." She waved her hand as if brushing something away. "I feel like an idiot."

"It happens," Sally said, grinning. "You and Jack Neville, huh? I never would've guessed."

"It's not funny," Vera said.

"I didn't mean to imply that it was. And I'm glad you came by. Now you know you don't have to worry about any competition from me. I like Jack very much, and I'm trying to help him a little with a problem, but we're just friends. I'm sure that's all we'll ever be."

"I don't have any men friends," Vera said. "Women, either. I think I come on too strong."

"Mae's your friend," Sally said.

"She puts up with me."

"Hey, it's a start."

"This thing you're helping Jack with," Vera said. "Could I help, too? Maybe he'd like me more if I did something for him."

Sally thought Jack would probably pass out if he knew that Vera Vaughn had designs on him. On the other hand, maybe he wouldn't.

"The police think Jack killed Ralph Bostic," Sally said.

Vera snorted. "Ridiculous. He'd never do that."

"I know. It was someone else, and I think I know who."

Vera looked interested. "Are you going to tell me?"

Why not? Sally thought.

"Come on back and let me warm up your coffee," she said. "I'll tell you all about it."

33

Sally's recitation took a cup and a half of coffee. When it was over, Vera said, "That's really very interesting, and I know you were quite the hero when you figured out who killed Val Hurley, but I think you're wrong this time."

"Why?" Sally asked. "Everything fits."

"Not quite," Vera said. "Hal Kaul might not make much more money than we do, but he doesn't need to. His wife has her own income."

"Enough to afford that huge new house?"

"She can afford whatever she wants. She was an only child, and when her father died two years ago, he left her the mineral rights to about twelve gas wells in East Texas. She probably gets more money every month than Hal makes in a year. Hal's living the ultimate male fantasy, being kept by a woman who's got a very nice income."

Now that they weren't talking about Jack, Sally thought, Vera had reverted to her old self. Sally thought she was wrong about that, however. While she wasn't at all sure what the ultimate male fantasy was, Sally would have been willing to bet it involved a Victoria's Secret model and some spiffy lingerie rather than money.

On the other hand, however, Vera might very well be right about Hal Kaul.

"With all that money coming in," Sally said, "Hal wouldn't be likely to be mixed up in some criminal scheme just for the fun of it. He has Internet auctions for entertainment."

"Typical male with his computer toy. He wouldn't risk that for the measly amount he could pick up on some scam to cheat the college out of auto-repair money."

Sally started to say that Jack Neville was addicted to playing games on his computer, but she thought better of it. Might as well let Vera find out for herself.

"If Hal didn't kill Bostic and Thomas," Sally said, "who did?"

"My money would be on Fieldstone," Vera said. "He's got the best motive. Bostic wanted him fired, and he was cheating the school besides. And then there's your friend Jorge."

"He wouldn't kill anyone."

"You said yourself you suspected him at first."

"Yes, but I don't think he had anything to do with it. I was certain it was Hal."

"You could ask him if he did it. He'd probably think it was funny."

"I don't think so," Sally said. "I'm just going to think everything through again and see if I get a different answer."

"We could work as a team. You could bounce ideas off me. I gave you a new perspective on Hal Kaul."

Sally had always thought of Vera as being more of a loner than a team player. But Vera was there, and she was eager to help.

"All right," Sally said. "Why not?"

Jack put on an allegedly rain-proof jacket that he'd ordered from Land's End and started out to his garage. He was almost to the door when he realized he couldn't actually go through with his plan. It would be great if it worked, but if it didn't, he might wind up dead. What would Sally think of him then? Probably that he had been crazy to have gone off alone to confront a man he believed to be a killer.

So he wouldn't go alone. He'd call Sally, explain his theory to her, and see if it matched whatever she had worked out for herself about the murders. Maybe they could put their ideas together and then go to Weems.

Or they could visit Owens. Whichever Sally thought was best.

Jack picked up his phone and had punched in Sally's number before he realized that there was no dial tone. That was typical, he thought. Whenever it rained, his phone was likely to go out. It had happened several times over the course of the last two or three years, and there was no telling when service would be restored.

One of these days, he thought, he was going to have to get a cell phone, as much as he hated them. As far as he was concerned, they were more of a nuisance than anything. He didn't like people who used them in cars, he didn't like people who used them in restaurants, and he really, *really* didn't like people who used them in movies. Still, it would certainly be nice to have one in a genuine emergency.

Jack looked out the window, still holding the useless telephone. The rain hadn't stopped. You could never be sure about rain when you lived near the Gulf. It might rain for an hour, or it might rain for days.

Maybe the fact that the phone didn't work was a sign, he thought. Maybe he couldn't get in touch with Sally because he was meant to go one-on-one with Stanley Owens and settle things that way. It was crazy, but what the heck.

On the other hand, he could just drive by Sally's house and pick her up.

He heard a noise in his garage. *Hector*, he thought. Although the cat would never deign to come inside the house, Jack liked to leave the garage door up about eight inches so that Hector could slip under it and have some shelter when it rained. Unfortunately, while Hector wasn't the least averse to keeping dry, he didn't know much about how to behave in enclosed spaces, especially one like Jack's garage, which presented him with a number of temptations to explore. This time he'd probably turned over the cardboard box that Jack used as a recycling bin, putting old newspapers in it until he could remember to dispose of them properly.

Jack went to the garage door. Maybe just this once, Hector would like to come inside. It seemed highly unlikely, but Jack was willing to risk it if Hector was.

Jack opened the door, and looked out into the garage. There was no sign of the cat, but then it was dark in there. What with the clouds and rain, not much light was getting in though the small glass windows or the crack under the door.

"Hector?" Jack said.

He was reaching for the light switch when someone stepped out of the shadows beside him and stuck something very sharp up under his chin.

"Aren't you going to invite me in, Neville?" Stanley Owens asked.

"I don't think it could be Talon," Vera said. "He has an awfully good alibi. I still think it's Fieldstone."

"I get the impression you don't like him," Sally said.

"That's not true. He's okay for an administrator."

Damning with faint praise, Sally thought.

"I just can't think of anyone else who might have done it," Vera continued. "There's no one else with a motive, unless you count Jorge."

"We're not counting him," Sally said.

"Right," Vera said.

They had been over the whole sequence of events again, and Sally was sure she hadn't left anything out. Vera had been eager to help, but she hadn't spotted anything Sally had missed.

There had to be something, though. Sally was sure of it. But what?

"Shouldn't we just call the police?" Vera asked. "They're really the ones who should be doing all this."

Sally told Vera about Weems and explained why calling the police wasn't the best of options.

"Typical of the male power structure," Vera said. "Men in positions of authority never listen to women. It's a terrible injustice. If a man takes a car in for repair, for example, the mechanic always accepts his word for what's wrong, but if a woman takes in the same car—"

"Hold it," Sally said.

Vera's discussion of auto repair had given Sally the answer. It had come to her just as quickly as it had to Jack.

"We have to go," she said.

"Where?" Vera asked.

"To see Mae."

"Why?"

"The killer has already eliminated two people who could implicate him in a crime. Both of them were going with Mae. What if one of them talked?"

"Mae would have told me," Vera said. "She didn't know anything."

Vera looked almost frightened, another sight Sally had never thought she'd see.

"The killer won't know that," Sally said.

"What about Jack?"

"We'll go by and see him later. Right now, we need to check on Mae."

"Call her," Vera said. "We could call Jack, too. There's no need to go by and see him."

"This isn't the eighth grade, Vera. It's not as if we're planning to ring his doorbell and then run and hide."

Vera blushed again. Twice in one day. Sally wished she had a witness. No one would believe her if she told anyone about it, not that she would. *Troy Beauchamp would love to know, however,* she thought. *Good grief. Maybe we never do really get out of the eighth grade.*

"Do you want to come along or not?" she asked Vera.

"I suppose so. You aren't going to say anything? To Jack?"

"About you? No. Just about Stanley Owens."

"What does he have to do with this?"

Sally told her.

"It makes a lot more sense than what you said about Hal," Vera said. "Mae has to be told. Calling would be quicker than going over there. I'll do it."

"Good idea," Sally said.

34

Owens stepped behind Jack, twisted his left arm up behind him, and backed him into the house, the point of his knife still sticking Jack under the chin. Jack almost screamed when Owens jerked his arm, not just because of the pain in the arm but because of the pain in his ribs. It was almost like being stabbed, but Jack knew that stabbing would be even more painful.

Although he couldn't see the knife Owens was holding, Jack was sure it was a very nice one, no doubt one of Owens's own custom jobs, all of which were superior to the knife Jack had made by several orders of magnitude. And sharper, too. Much sharper.

Jack had his head tilted back, but he couldn't tilt it back far enough to get it away from the knife, which had made a small puncture in the skin. There was a thin trickle of blood running down his neck.

Following right along behind them as they went into the den came Hector.

"That's a nice cat you have," Owens said. "Real friendly."

Great, Jack thought. *Just great. For the first time in his life Hector decides to associate a little bit with a human being, and he picks a killer.* Jack was bitterly disappointed in Hector's judgment, but Hector didn't seem to care in the least. He walked about the house, sniffing around the bottoms of chairs and at small spots on the rug. Then he wandered off and out of Jack's restricted field of vision.

Owens forgot about him. So did Jack. The point of the knife was focusing his attention elsewhere.

"I guess I talked a little too much this morning, didn't I, Neville?" Owens said.

Jack couldn't very well nod, and he didn't feel like talking, either. It would be painful to open his mouth, what with the point of the knife poking him where it was.

"That's all right," Owens said. "You don't have to answer. I know I did. I didn't realize it until about half an hour ago, and when I did, I thought I'd better pay you a visit. You'd figured it out, hadn't you? Because I'm going to feel like a real idiot if you hadn't."

Jack still couldn't respond, so Owens moved the knife a fraction of an inch.

"Yes," Jack said. "I'd figured it out."

"Doesn't really matter," Owens said, giving Jack a little jab. "You'd know now, wouldn't you?"

What Jack knew was that he'd been completely out of his mind ever to consider paying Owens a visit alone. If he had it to do all over again, he'd take a division of marines. Because he certainly wasn't capable of dealing with Owens at all.

John Wayne would have been a different story. Big John would have disarmed Owens and stabbed him to death with his own knife.

Or he would have shot him with a pistol that he happened to have lying around the house, or concealed in his boot.

Jack, however, wasn't John Wayne. He wasn't wearing boots, and he didn't have a pistol lying around the house.

Score one for the NRA, Jack thought. Even Sally had a pistol around the house, while all he had was an old softball bat that he'd used as a kid and that he now kept in the bedroom in case of a home invasion. The handle of the bat was cracked, and there was tape wrapped around it to hold it together, so it might not have been much of a defense. Jack would have liked to try it, though, just to see how hard he could hit Owens in the head, broken bat or not.

"I really wish I'd kept my mouth shut today," Owens said. "I guess seeing you at the dealership shocked me a little bit. I thought you'd be in jail for sure by now. When I stuck your knife in Bostic, I thought you'd be in jail within a day. But the cops never can figure things out. So I guess we're going to have to help them."

Jack didn't ask how. He wouldn't have asked even if he could have. He had a feeling he didn't want to know.

But Owens told him anyway.

"You're going to have to kill yourself," he said. "After expressing remorse and all that stuff. It's always better when there's a note expressing remorse. People these days go for that kind of thing."

Jack was pretty sure Owens didn't have a clue as to what remorse really was. If anything, Owens seemed to be enjoying himself.

"You'll need to explain how you were sorry that you killed Bostic and Thomas, but they were robbing the school, and it didn't look like anyone was going to stop them, so you just took matters into your own hands."

"No notes," Jack mumbled, or tried to. It wasn't easy with the knife poking him. "People will know they're fake."

Owens seemed to understand him and eased off on the pressure of the knife.

"Nobody's going to know that. After all, I haven't been here."

"You're here. How'd you get in?"

"You shouldn't leave your garage door up so high. I slid right under it. And don't worry about anybody seeing my car. It's parked down the street in the parking lot of a 24/7 Mart. Nobody will notice it at all."

Jack thought someone might have noticed a man walking down the street in the rain, but that wasn't such an unusual sight in Hughes.

"Now," Owens said, "about your suicide. Do you have any preferences?"

Oddly enough, Jack couldn't think of a single one.

"Don't worry," Owens said. "I'll come up with something. Maybe you could just have an accident instead. That might be better. How does electrocution in the bathtub sound to you?"

Jack didn't own a hair dryer or a small radio that plugged in. He wondered if Owens would try throwing the stereo into the bathtub. It wouldn't fit very well, and it certainly wouldn't look like an accident, not unless the cops thought Jack was trying to wash it.

"Maybe you could get your hand caught in the garbage disposal," Owens said. "You could chop it up and bleed to death."

Jack didn't like that idea any more than he'd liked the first one. Less, if anything. It sounded a good deal more painful. In fact, he didn't like the idea of dying at all, which came as no big surprise to him. Sally might not want to go out with him, but he had plenty to live for. He had to finish his article about the Kingston Trio. And he wanted to play a few more games of Freecell.

"I think I like electrocution better," Owens said thoughtfully. "Where do you keep your hair dryer?"

Jack didn't answer right away, so Owens gave him a little jab with the knife point.

"I don't have one," Jack said.

Owens laughed. "Good try. But I know better than that. Everybody has a hair dryer around the house."

"Not me," Jack said.

Owens gigged him with the knife and jerked Jack's arm up. Jack winced, bit back a scream, and tried to pretend it didn't hurt. He wasn't very successful.

"Don't give me that crap, Neville," Owens said. "Show me where it is."

"I really don't have one," Jack said when Owens moved the knife away. "You can look all you want, but you won't find one."

"I guess it doesn't matter," Owens said. "I'd just have to undress you to put you in the tub. I wasn't looking forward to that part anyway. We'll have to think of something else."

Jack loved that *we*. He certainly wasn't going to think of anything. Let Owens worry about it.

"Autoerotic death," Owens said. "I like the idea of that. Poetic justice, right?"

Jack tried to say he didn't get the point.

"Auto," Owens said. "Pretty funny. We had us a sweet little deal going until you stirred things up. Cars go to Mexico, drugs come back, everybody makes money. But you had Bostic on the run, and Thomas was scared to death."

Jack found it hard to believe that he'd scared anyone, but he knew the deal was about to come unraveled, and maybe he'd contributed. He didn't think Thomas had been scared to death, however, and he said so.

"No, that was pretty much an accident," Owens said. "And then you and your friend came nosing around. I should have finished you off right then. Now it's going to be more complicated. The way we'll do it is that we'll get out one of your old *Playboy* magazines. Maybe a *Penthouse*. *Hustler* would be even better. You'll strangle yourself with your own belt while you're looking at them and playing with yourself. Where do you keep 'em?"

Jack said, "I don't have any magazines like that. How about *The New Republic*?"

"The new *what*? Jesus Christ, don't tell me you don't have any girlie magazines around!"

It was true. Jack restricted his reading to other kinds of magazines, though he did watch an R-rated movie on cable now and then.

"You're turning out to be more trouble than you're worth," Owens said, "and I think you're a liar besides. Where's the bathroom?"

Jack pointed with his right hand.

"Let's go, then," Owens said. "I think I'll find a hair dryer in there, don't you?"

Jack didn't think so, not unless someone had sneaked one in while he wasn't looking. But let Owens search for it. Jack would use the time to come up with a clever plan to escape.

Or he would have used the time that way if he could only think clearly. All that really came to him was that the knife was really hurting his chin and that his arm felt as if it were about to come apart at the shoulder socket and that his ribs felt as if they might be splintering into his lungs. Aside from that, however, he was doing just fine.

"My chin," he tried to say as Owens marched him toward the master bedroom.

"What's that?" Owens asked, moving the knife a bit.

"My chin," Jack told him. "It's going to have a hole in it. If you kill me, the cops will wonder how it got there."

Owens stopped. He obviously hadn't thought of that.

"Besides," Jack said, "the woman who was with me this morning knows you killed Bostic and Thomas. She saw your face yesterday in the auto shop. She's probably on her way to the police right now."

"Ha ha," Owens said flatly. "You'll have to do better than that, Neville. If you haven't called the cops yet, I know she hasn't. Women can't figure stuff like that out. Look how long it took you. I thought about her seeing me, though, and I decided that she didn't. When the cops didn't show up at the dealership today, I knew she hadn't. Hey, if she'd seen me, then I'd have to kill her, wouldn't I? And you don't want that. Or do you?"

Jack definitely didn't want that, so he didn't mention that Sally had already solved one murder.

"Of course you couldn't very well have called the cops or any-body else," Owens said. "What with your telephone line down in your backyard. That wind and rain do terrible things."

Jack had a feeling it hadn't been the wind or the rain that had affected his phone line this time, not that it mattered. It had hap-pened so often before that no one would question it.

"Did you call here last night?" he asked.

"Spooked you, huh?" Owens said. "I was just checking up in case I needed to get to you, but I figured I could wait. And now we've talked enough. Come on. I'm not worried about that cut under your chin. When they find out that you've electrocuted yourself, maybe they'll think you tried cutting your throat and just chickened out. You're the kind who would."

That remark really bothered Jack, and he would have said something if it hadn't been so close to the truth. He wasn't the kind to kill himself, and everyone was going to know it, no matter how good Owens made things look. He didn't see the point of trying to explain that to Owens, who wouldn't listen anyway. He heard only what he wanted to hear.

The bathroom adjoined the master bedroom, and the door was open. Owens dragged Jack over to the bathroom and looked around. There was no hair dryer, but there was something else that Owens noticed.

"Nice terry-cloth robe," he said.

He did something with the knife. It disappeared from beneath Jack's chin, and Jack relaxed slightly. Owens kept Jack's arm twisted, so there was no chance to break away.

Still holding Jack firmly, Owens used his free hand to pull the robe off the hook where it was hanging.

"Did you steal this at a good hotel, or did you spend money for it?" he asked.

Jack didn't bother to answer. Owens yanked the cloth belt from its loops and threw the robe on the bed.

"I'm going to tie you up while I find that hair dryer," he said. "This cloth won't leave any marks."

He reached for Jack's free arm, and in doing so he eased the pressure on the left. Jack pulled his right arm away, did a half-spin, and tried to hit Owens with a balled fist.

Owens still had a grip on Jack's left arm, and he nearly pulled it off, or so it seemed to Jack. Owens slammed Jack in the back of the head with the heel of his hand.

The blow rattled Jack's teeth and sent him stumbling across the room. He hit the edge of the bed and fell facedown across it. Before he could get up, Owens came over with the belt in his hand.

"Hold still," Owens said, "or I'll hit you again."

Owens stood against the bed, straddling Jack and pinning him in place. He pulled Jack's arms behind his back and began to tie Jack's wrists together.

Then two things happened: The doorbell rang, and Owens jerked backward, screaming.

When he felt Owens's grip relax, Jack didn't waste time trying to figure out what was going on. He rolled off the end of the bed, crabbed around to the other side, and grabbed his softball bat.

He rolled over just in time to see Owens flying through the air toward him, knife poised to plunge into some tender part of Jack's anatomy, of which there were plenty.

Jack swung the bat up from the floor, hoping to split Owens's face down the middle, but the result was much less satisfactory than Jack had hoped. It was, however, along the lines that Jack should have expected. He'd never been a very good hitter in his faraway softball days, and instead of connecting with Owens's head, the bat struck his shoulder.

Luckily, it was the right shoulder, and Owens was right-handed. He dropped the knife just before he landed squarely on top of Jack.

Jack shoved him off and grabbed for the knife, which had landed just at the edge of the bed. He almost had it when Owens's hand closed around his wrist.

Jack never exercised his forearm except when he used the computer mouse to play Freecell, so he wasn't exactly muscular. Owens didn't have any trouble at all moving Jack's hand away from the knife and then taking it. He sat straddling Jack, looking down into his eyes, and holding the knife blade at his throat.

"You know something?" Owens said.

Jack didn't dare nod. He had a feeling that if he did, he'd cut his own throat, which was probably what Owens was hoping for. Jack wasn't going to give him the satisfaction.

"This is a really sharp knife," Owens said when Jack didn't respond. "You could shave with it better than you could with a razor blade."

Jack didn't doubt it. The knife Bowie had made in *The Iron Mistress* couldn't have been any sharper.

"People talk about knife makers like Bradshaw and Lightfoot," Owens said, "but I'm as good as those guys. I can teach other people how to make good knives, and I enjoy doing it. I sort of hate to use one to kill a person with."

Jack wondered if Owens would appreciate a little lesson on how to avoid ending a sentence with a preposition. Probably not.

"I really wish you hadn't taken that class, Neville," Owens continued. "I thought it would be easy to frame you, but it's turned out to be almost more trouble than it's worth. You wouldn't even commit. You didn't even want to have an accident. And you know what that means."

Jack wasn't one hundred percent certain, but he was afraid he had a pretty good idea.

Owens confirmed it.

"Since you won't cooperate, I'll just have to kill you myself."

Jack had no doubt that Owens meant it, and there wasn't a thing Jack could do about it. He took a deep breath and waited for his generally uneventful life to flash before his eyes.

He didn't think it would take very long.

35

Before Jack's life had flashed anywhere, however, Sally Good walked through the bedroom door and pointed her pistol at Owens's head.

"I wouldn't kill him if I were you," she told Owens. "Too many witnesses."

"That's right," Vera Vaughn said from over Sally's shoulder. "We're all watching."

"And besides," Sally said, "I have a pistol."

Owens didn't seem impressed. He looked at Sally coldly and didn't move for quite some time.

"If I don't kill him," he said finally, "you'll have to let me leave here."

"Let Jack up and we'll talk it over," Sally said.

She didn't know what she would do if Owens refused. Faced with the possibility that she might have to pull the trigger on another human being, she still wasn't sure that she could do it, even if it meant Jack's life. She hoped she wouldn't have to find out.

Owens sat quietly for a few interminable seconds. Then he stood up very slowly and turned away from Jack. Sally tried not to let her relief show.

"Put the pistol down," Owens said, "and let me walk out of here. Otherwise, I'm going to flip this knife right into Neville's heart."

Sally wasn't sure how easy that would be, but Owens appeared to be perfectly confident that he could do it.

"You put the knife down, and I'll put the pistol down," Sally said, thankful that she had an excuse not to shoot. "Put the knife on the nightstand, and I'll lay the pistol on the dresser."

Owens was watching her closely as she took a step toward the dresser, so he didn't see Jack rise up on his knees behind him, holding a softball bat.

Sally almost said something, but she bit off the words as the bat came down and landed squarely into the middle of Owens's back with a solid thud.

Owens went down like a sack of rocks and didn't move. Just to be sure that he was out, Sally went over to him and prodded him with her toe. He lay still, so she stuck the pistol barrel in his ear. Then she pinched his ear as hard as she could with her free hand. Owens remained still, and Sally stood up.

When she did, Hector streaked out from beneath the bed and sped out of the room, looking more like a blur than a cat.

"Who's that?" Sally asked.

"Hector," Jack said. "I think he tried to sever Owens's Achilles tendon. What do we do now?"

"Call nine-one-one," Sally said.

"My phone's out of order."

"I have a cell phone," Vera said.

She went into the den to make the call, and Mae Wilkins poked her head into the bedroom.

"Is everything all right?" she asked.

"Just fine," Sally said.

Mae looked at Owens and said, "Is that the man who killed Ralph and Ray?"

"I think so," Sally said.

"Is he dead?"

"Probably not."

"Too bad," Mae said, and left the room.

Weems arrived on the scene very quickly. That was the last thing that happened quickly, though. It took hours to get things straightened out to Weems's satisfaction, and Sally wasn't sure the detective was satisfied even then. Sally suspected that Weems was still looking for a way to blame Jack for something.

Since after Jack and Sally's explanation of all that had happened Weems could hardly blame Jack for the murders, the detective decided to settle for the next best things: guilt and blame.

"We nearly had this all wrapped up," he said. "There were a couple of guys going after it from the stolen cars angle, and we were just about ready to tie that to the murders. You could have spoiled everything."

Sally didn't ask him how he knew that. She didn't think Weems would have an answer anyway, mainly because she didn't believe half of what he said about being ready to tie things together.

"You can see what happens when amateurs interfere with an official investigation," Weems continued, looking at Jack. "Something bad always happens. Neville here nearly got himself killed."

"I didn't, though," Jack said, although Weems certainly had a point. Jack's ribs were killing him, and he could still feel the knife on his throat. "Sally came through again."

Jack probably shouldn't have added that *again*, Sally thought. It was just a reminder to Weems that it was the second time that Sally (and Jack, apparently) had come up with an answer that Weems hadn't been able to find.

Weems said that everyone would have to come to the police station and make a statement, and he and the other cops finally left. Sally wasn't sorry to see them leave. They had taken Owens away long ago, after he'd recovered consciousness.

"Anyone want something to drink?" Jack asked when the police had cleared out.

Nobody did.

"I'm glad you brought the pistol, Sally," Jack said. "How did you know Owens was here?"

"I didn't know," she told him. "I thought he was at Mae's, so

Vera and I went to check. Then we decided to drive by here, just in case. You should probably lock your front door, you know."

"People would just slide under the garage door," Jack said. "That's what Owens did. When did you figure out that he was the killer?"

"This morning," Sally said. "How about you?"

"It was a couple of hours ago, but it was too late to do any good. By then he was already here."

Vera was eyeing Jack oddly. Sally wondered what she was thinking.

"I'm glad we came by," Vera said to Jack. "I wouldn't want anything to happen to you."

Jack looked askance at Sally, who grinned and shrugged.

"Owens would have escaped if it hadn't been for you," Vera continued.

Sally wondered if Vera was right. Sally thought she might have been able to use the pistol, but she still wasn't sure. She might have simply let Owens walk out of the house. It was just as well they hadn't had to find out.

"It was really brave of you to hit him with the bat," Vera told Jack.

"Well, pilgrim," Jack said, in what Sally thought was a John Wayne imitation somewhat inferior to her own, "a man's gotta do what a man's gotta do."

Sally spent the evening at home with Lola. Sally used the time to read a book, while Lola sat on her lap and shed hairs all over both Sally's pants and the couch. Once Lola even purred.

Sally didn't know where Jack was, but she suspected that Vera might very well have proposed that the two of them go out and do something together. Sally wondered how Jack would respond to an offer like that. She hoped that if he accepted, he was up to whatever demands Vera might make on him. After all, he had to teach class on Monday. Sally had called Fieldstone and Naylor and made sure of that.

As for Jorge and Mae, Sally just tried not to think about them. It wasn't any of her business. If Jorge wanted to date a woman whose house looked as it had just been sterilized, that was up to him, though she wasn't sure that Jorge was grimy enough for Mae.

The telephone rang, and Lola sank her claws into Sally's thighs before jumping off and running to hide under the bed.

Sally picked up the phone and said hello.

"Hello," said her mother. "I heard on the news that they caught that awful murderer in Hughes. Some policeman named Weems was interviewed, and he said something about diligent police work. I'm glad you live in a community where the police do such good work. And I'm really glad you didn't get mixed up in things this time."

"Me, too," Sally said.